# Kitchen Chaos

# *the* SATURDAY COOKING CLUB

## Kitchen Chaos

Deborah A. Levine *and* JillEllyn Riley

**ALADDIN**

NEW YORK   LONDON   TORONTO   SYDNEY   NEW DELHI

This book is a work of fiction. Any references to historical events, real people, or real places are used fictitiously. Other names, characters, places, and events are products of the authors' imagination, and any resemblance to actual events or places or persons, living or dead, is entirely coincidental.

## ALADDIN

An imprint of Simon & Schuster Children's Publishing Division
1230 Avenue of the Americas, New York, NY 10020
First Aladdin hardcover edition February 2015
Text copyright © 2015 by Deborah A. Levine and JillEllyn Riley
Jacket illustrations copyright © 2015 by Leo Espinosa
Also available in an Aladdin paperback edition.
For information about special discounts for bulk purchases,
please contact Simon & Schuster Special Sales at 1-866-506-1949
or business@simonandschuster.com.
The Simon and Schuster Speakers Bureau can bring authors to your live event. For
more information or to book an event, contact the Simon & Schuster Speakers
Bureau at 1-866-248-3049 or visit our website at www.simonspeakers.com.
The text of this book was set in Arno Pro.
Jacket designed by Jessica Handelman
Interior designed by Mike Rosamilia
Manufactured in the United States of America 0115 FFG
2 4 6 8 10 9 7 5 3 1
Library of Congress Control Number 2014935944
ISBN 978-1-4424-9939-3 (hc)
ISBN 978-1-4424-9940-9 (pbk)
ISBN 978-1-4424-9941-6 (eBook)

*For L, my number-one Brooklyn girl,*
*and all of the fierce and lovely friends who*
*have brightened our world.—DAL*

*For my beloved grandmothers,*
*Frances Jane Clark Brown and Dorothy Roberts Riley.*
*One loved to cook and the other cooked for love . . .*
*both inspired the girls around them.—JER*

*Kitchen Chaos*

# CHAPTER 1
## *Liza*

Whoever invented school lunch must have really hated kids. Or at least not wanted us to eat. The sad-looking, blah-colored lunchroom walls alone are enough to make you lose your appetite. Then there's the smell—greasy tater tots, sour milk, and that bucket full of moldy, cloudy water the custodian keeps in the corner with the mop. And don't get me started on the food. I mean, what could be more depressing than a soggy taco? A limp burrito is one thing—at least they're supposed to be sort of mushy. But tacos are supposed to be crunchy, right?

I'm pondering this and trying to figure out how to take a bite of my leaky lunch, while across the table my best friend, Frankie, is digging into some tasty-looking pasta she brought from home. Frankie's dad makes these amazing family dinners, and she always brings the leftovers for lunch. Meanwhile, I'm stuck with the school lunch plan since my mom's too busy these days to go grocery shopping, let alone cook. Last year we did a unit on the justice system in social studies, and looking at Frankie's lunch next to mine, one thing is clear: There is no justice in the school cafeteria.

"You're not seriously going to eat that, are you?" Frankie asks, practically hollering over the dull roar of yelling kids, screeching chairs, and the random CD mixes our music teacher, Mr. Jackson, puts on every day at lunch (today's is Broadway/hip-hop/Latin jazz, I think). "It looks like they scooped the leftovers out of Rocco's bowl and wrapped them in a used tortilla."

Rocco is Frankie's pug, and I bet even he'd turn up his pushed-in little nose at the contents of my taco. Thankfully, Frankie starts spooning half of her penne into the empty rectangle on my lunch tray.

"Thanks, Franks. I would starve without you," I say, grateful that my best friend is generous *and* well fed.

"I know," Frankie says with a grin. "It's exhausting to be so kind and generous all the time, but it's just my way."

I gently kick her under the table and eagerly dive into my pasta. Even cold, it's tastier than anything the Clinton Middle School lunch ladies have to offer. Not that it's their fault—they don't make the slop, they just heat it up and plop it down on our trays. They probably bring their own lunch from home, just like Frankie and every other sane person at Clinton.

Out of nowhere, Frankie throws her fork down on the table and starts bouncing up and down like she just sat on a hairbrush. She looks so ridiculous, I almost spit out my last bite of pasta because I'm laughing so hard.

"What's up?" I manage to ask, holding my hand over my mouth and trying to swallow.

Frankie leans over and grabs my arm, dramatically. "Today is Tuesday!"

"Um, okay," I say. "And tomorrow is Wednesday. Then comes Thursday. . . . "

Frankie rolls her eyes. "Liza," she sighs, "we have a double period of social studies on Tuesdays." She's bouncing again.

Our social studies teacher, Mr. McEnroe, is tall and green-eyed with long, sandy hair that he wears in a ponytail. He's really young (you know, for a teacher) and looks sort of like a brainy surfer. Frankie has a major "secret" crush on him that's completely obvious to everyone who knows her. I'm not boy crazy like she is, but even I have to admit he's pretty cute.

"You're insane," I tell Frankie, who is packing up her lunch so fast, you'd think there was a clean-table competition or something. On Tuesdays we have social studies right after lunch, and Frankie says she likes to get there early because it's her favorite class, but I know she just wants to spy on Mr. McEnroe through the door while he gets ready. I usually go along with her, even though I think she's nuts. Someday I'll do something she thinks is crazy too, and I'll want her to stick by me, won't I?

"C'mon!" Frankie calls out to me. She's already halfway up the stairs to the second floor, and I'm still jogging down the empty main hallway past the library and the eighth-grade gym. I can hear my own shoes squeak because we're the only ones here. I finally catch up to her by the water fountain that is just down the hall from Mr. Mac's room. I take a much-needed gulp of water while Frankie sneaks closer to the door. When I look up from the fountain, I see that for the first time ever, the door to Mr. McEnroe's room is already open. Frankie nearly faints when he pokes his head out and smiles as if he were expecting us.

"Hello, girls," he says. "Right on time as usual."

Actually, we're thirteen minutes early, but I appreciate Mr. McEnroe not making us feel like total geeks. He's not clueless, so I'm sure by now he's figured out why we're always so "on time" for class.

"I've got something pretty exciting for you guys to get started on today," he tells us as we settle into our desks in the totally empty classroom and take out our notebooks.

"What is it?" Frankie asks with a little too much enthusiasm. "Another field trip?" It's only the first week of October, and we've already gone on two social studies field trips.

"Not this time, Francesca," Mr. McEnroe says. Frankie blushes a little whenever he calls her by her full name like that. "Today I'm going to assign the class your first project."

Another good thing about Mr. McEnroe is that he's really big on us working together— "collaboratively," he calls it—so we're never just sitting silently at our desks while he drones on and on. I'm a pretty good student, but I don't know how some teachers can expect us to pay attention for a full forty-five minutes while they just blab about something even they don't seem to care about. I love working on projects, though, especially with Frankie, because when it comes to the creative stuff, like brainstorming ideas and making posters or dioramas, it's as if the two of us are somehow sharing a single brain.

Mr. McEnroe watches as Frankie and I turn and give each other a silent fist bump. Okay, maybe we are a little geeky about class projects. "Liza and I are partners, right?" Frankie asks.

The two of us are partners for pretty much

everything. In P.E., I count to twenty while Frankie does crunches, and she holds the rope while I huff and puff my way to the top (okay, more like the middle). In Spanish we quiz each other on verb tenses, and once we even made up a little skit called "Las Señoritas Bonitas" and put on wigs, makeup, and these really poofy dresses that looked completely ridiculous and not at all *bonita*. My mom still shows her friends the video of us demonstrating how to make a banana smoothie back in third grade—we were so nervous, we forgot to peel the banana.

"Well," Mr. McEnroe says, turning a chair around and straddling it backward like boys always do, "that depends."

Frankie and I freeze mid–fist bump and exchange another look, only this time we're more confused than excited. "What do you mean?" I ask. "Depends on what?"

"I know you two like to work together, but I've decided the class will be working in groups of three for this project. So, you girls can collaborate, but you're going to have to find a third partner, too. You may be the Dynamic Duo, but being part of a team is a great skill to learn."

Frankie and I look pleadingly at Mr. McEnroe. "But—," we both say at exactly the same time, but Mr. Mac just smiles at us and shakes his head.

"Cheer up, girls," he says, still grinning and getting up from his chair. "Sometimes you have to stir things up."

Just then the bell rings and the rest of the class starts filing in.

# CHAPTER 2
## *Frankie*

Dylan Davis has greasy hair and one of those skinny little almost-mustaches that's too thin to start shaving but just obvious enough that you can't stop staring at it. At least I can't. I have two older brothers (better known as "The Goons") who are far from babe-magnet material—but at least they never had cheesy-looking facial hair like Dylan's. For the next fifteen minutes I'm stuck staring at the 'stache because Mr. Mac told us to pair up with the person sitting across from us, and for me, that meant Dylan. Our new unit is on immigration, and our first assignment is to "interview" our partners about where their ancestors lived before they came to America.

"So, uh, where are your, uh, ancestors from?" Dylan asks me. Actually, he reads the question straight from his notebook, and I'm pretty sure he doesn't even know what "ancestor" means. The only thing less appealing about Dylan Davis than his looks is his personality. He doesn't actually have one from what I can tell.

"Italy," I say automatically, because I know this history so well. Family lore and all that. "Sicily to be exact. My grandparents came to Brooklyn straight from there—both sides."

Both sets of my grandparents arrived in Brooklyn from Sicily right after they got married, and our family has lived in Carroll Gardens ever since. My grandparents have been New Yorkers for something like fifty years, but they still have such heavy Sicilian accents, you'd think they just got here last week.

I can tell Dylan is not remotely interested, so I look him directly in the eye, because I know it makes him nervous. My turn: "How about you?"

Dylan picks at his already-ragged cuticles. "I, uh, I'm not sure. My granddad's parents were from England, I think. He has a picture of one of those flag things with the messed up X over his desk."

"You mean the Union Jack?" I ask. I know I shouldn't make him feel dumb, but can I help if he does? No.

"Yeah, I guess," he says. "I don't really know where anyone else is from. My mom's family and my dad's family don't get along, so we don't see our relatives very much or anything."

I can't even imagine what that would be like. At my house it's all family, all the time. There are six of us—my mom, my dad, my three brothers, and me—and both of my parents come from big families too.

I have twenty-seven first cousins, no joke. Having so much family around all the time can be seriously annoying, but at least my people aren't in a feud. And there's always some drama somewhere with some member of the family, so it keeps things interesting. I'd almost feel sorry for Dylan if he weren't so boring.

"You're probably going to have to find out more about your ancestors for the project," I tell him. Mr. McEnroe explained the project in his usual smart, funny way right before he had us pair up to do these interviews. He can make anything appealing—at least to me. I hope I don't let it show. He gave us a handout that said, *American Immigration: Wave upon Wave Arriving at Our Shores* (only Mr. Mac can get away with nerdy assignments like that!) and told us that at different points in American history, people moved to the United States in groups, or "waves," from all over the world. Sometimes they were welcomed, sometimes not. For our project we have to choose an aspect of immigration to study and present. We can do anything we want—as long as it includes a written report *and* a hands-on project. Then all of us seventh graders will present our projects in an "Immigration Museum" we create at the end of the unit, the week before Thanksgiving.

Those are the only instructions Mr. McEnroe gave us, which is kind of cool, but also a little stressful. When teachers say things like, "The only rule is that there are no rules" or "There is no right answer," they're usually not telling you the absolute truth. If you do a really lame job or come up with an answer that's completely out there, they're not just going to say, "Excellent work." They're going to make you do it again. I like to get things right the first time *and* have someone say, "Excellent work." So does Liza, which is another reason we make such a great team.

Since Mr. Mac is determined to have us work in groups of three, I start looking around the room for a third partner who's not a slacker. Luckily, the person we're interviewing doesn't have to be part of our project group. Dim-bulb Davis with his skeevy mustache definitely isn't a candidate. It will have to be someone who's smart and creative but won't try to take over when Liza and I come up with one of our brilliant ideas. None of our good friends are in the class, but I notice Maya Lutz and consider her a possibility. She's a decent student and seems like she'd be easy to work with. But in the next second I remember something and scratch Maya off my mental list. I've heard some kids call her "Lutz the Klutz," and she must have done something to earn the nickname. Klutziness is not a desirable quality in a project partner. That could be dangerous. I don't want to be mean, but I want to get a good grade, so forget Maya, no matter how nice she is.

I scan the room again and land on Evan Jacoby. Interesting. He's a hard worker—I think he might actually be taking notes on Arianna Martinez's family history—and he's been in love with Liza since sixth grade, so he'd definitely go along with whatever idea we come up with. He also lives right down the block from school, which would be super convenient for project planning. Liza might not be thrilled about teaming up with a guy who's been crushing on her for a year, but I'm sure I can convince her he's the right choice. I mean, who else is there?

I look over at Liza to let her know our problem is solved—we practically have ESP, so all I have to do is, like, raise my eyebrow and she'll get it—but she's still chatting away with her interview partner. Her name is Lillian, I think, and she's new. She didn't go to Clinton last year, so she must have moved or switched schools or something. To be honest, I'd hardly noticed Lillian until just now, and I can't imagine what they're still talking about. But Liza is always super friendly and asks a lot of questions. I think she learned how to connect well with people in that support group her mom and dad made her go to for kids dealing with divorce.

Dylan Davis and I, on the other hand, are pretty

much interviewed out, since he couldn't exactly answer any of my questions and does not seem inclined to ask me any more. Mr. Boring is apparently really into his cuticles, and I can't get Liza's attention, so I decide to take a good long look at Lillian. She's Asian American, with straight, practically black hair that covers almost half of her face when she doesn't tuck it behind her ears. She wears dark blue glasses, and her clothes are okay, but there's something about them that's a little too neat. Her jeans look sort of stiff, like they've been ironed or sent to the dry cleaner.

Whenever I get my hands on the remote—which, in a house with three brothers, isn't often!—my favorite thing to watch on TV is makeover shows. Right now I wish I were the stylist and Lillian the guest because I can think of at least twelve different things she could do to really improve her look.

She must have sensed someone was looking at her, because all of a sudden, Lillian turns around and catches me staring. Liza looks over too and smiles. I smile back and nod my head toward Evan Jacoby, but she just scrunches up her forehead. Something in the atmosphere must be interfering with our ESP. I'll have to wait till after class to tell her my perfect project partner solution.

# CHAPTER 3
## *Lillian*

"You know what, Lillian? You'd be the perfect third project partner," Liza practically squeals. "I can't wait to tell Frankie!"

We both look over at Liza's BFF, Frankie, who—weirdly—is staring right at us. Liza smiles and waves at her, so I do too, even though we don't really know each other. Frankie doesn't seem to even notice me as she waves at Liza. It isn't really surprising. I'm in two classes with Frankie, and she's never spoken a word to me. I have the same two classes with Liza—social studies and math—and she always says "hi" when we pass in the hall, but this is the first time we've ever talked. She's really nice, and I hope she means it about being project partners with them.

"Okay," announces Liza with purpose, bringing my attention back to her. "Now it's your turn to talk about your ancestors."

Liza just finished telling me her family's story. Her mom grew up in Atlanta, but she says her relatives got lucky and found some really good records, so they can trace her ancestors back to Africa, before they were brought to America as slaves. She said her dad's relatives fled eastern Europe along with a lot of other Jewish families who were treated unfairly or forced to leave around the beginning of the last century. I guess on both sides, Liza's ancestors had a lot to overcome. My family history in the United States is a lot less interesting—and shorter—than hers.

Mr. McEnroe mentioned something about a first wave of immigrants from China to America during the nineteenth century, but that was long before my parents came. They're actually not even citizens—which is perfectly fine with them—but since my sister, Katie, and I were born here, we're officially Americans.

"Um, so, both of my parents were born in China and grew up there," I say. "They even got married there. Then, about twenty years ago, they moved to Berkeley to go to graduate school. They had a lot of relatives in San Francisco, and when they got jobs, they decided to stay. A few years later, my sister was born, and then me. That's pretty much the whole story, unless you count moving here this summer."

"Wow," Liza says. "That's a pretty short story." She smiles. "So does your family miss China? Do they talk about it?"

"Yeah," I say. "A lot, actually. I mean, back home in San Francisco, China seemed really close. With all of my aunts, uncles, and cousins and my grand-mother around, somebody was always going back to visit, bringing us stuff, talking about what's going on. I've been to China only a few times, but my parents go almost every year. Even though they've lived in the U.S. for so long, they don't really like American music or TV or anything. They think Chinese things are better."

"Your family sounds a lot like Frankie's," says Liza. "My mom has only one sister and my dad's an only child, so I just have my grandparents and the one aunt. I don't even have any cousins. You and Frankie are lucky to have so many people around all the time."

"I guess," I say, looking down at my hands. "Only they're all back in San Francisco."

"Oh yeah," says Liza, sounding sorry. "That must be hard." She pauses, but I don't feel like explaining how many hours a day I spend thinking about my cousin Chloe and my best friend, Sierra, so I don't say anything.

Liza changes the subject. "So, what do you think of Brooklyn?"

I shrug. "I'm still sort of getting used to it."

"I've never been to San Francisco," Liza says. "But I've heard it's really cool. Lots of hills, right? And the Golden Gate Bridge or something?"

I nod.

"Brooklyn's cool too," she assures me. "You'll see."

Just then the classroom lights flick on and off, which means Mr. McEnroe wants us to wrap things up. My fifth-grade teacher used to do that. It's funny how right now, thousands of miles away from each other, two teachers might be signaling their class to finish their work in exactly the same way. I think about Sierra and Chloe and wonder whether they're in social studies too.

"Okay, everyone, I'm going to need your attention for a minute," Mr. McEnroe says. "I hope you found this interview exercise enlightening. I went around the room listening to your conversations, and if my notes are correct, as a class we emigrated from twenty-six different countries—including Scotland and Ireland, where my own ancestors hail from. Pretty exciting, huh?"

I'm not sure whether we're supposed to answer him or not, because I still haven't totally figured Mr. McEnroe out. He seems like a really cool teacher, but I wonder what everyone else thinks. I look around to see what the other kids are doing. Just nodding. I can do that too.

"Now it's time to partner up in groups of three for the project I introduced earlier. Do you think you can handle dividing up with a minimum of drama, or do I need to do it for you?"

"We can handle it!" everyone seems to say at the same time—except for me, since I've been dreading this moment since the beginning of class. Did Liza mean what she said earlier, or was she just being nice?

"All right." Mr. McEnroe rubs his hands together,

smiling. "You have five minutes. And remember: Best friends don't necessarily make the best collaborators."

I'm starting to get a feeling in my stomach like I might throw up when I feel a tug on my sweater.

It's Liza. "Hey," she says. "Come on. Let's go tell Frankie you're going to be our third group member."

Suddenly, the awful feeling disappears. I smile at Liza and follow her over to Frankie, who's talking to a boy named Evan.

# CHAPTER 4
## *Liza*

I have to give it to Frankie, she doesn't mess around. As my nana would say, she "doesn't let the grass grow under her feet" (whatever that means). She's already practically interrogating this kid Evan, who just looks dazed and keeps nervously nodding.

"So you don't have that much going on after school, right? We can work on this as much as we want?" I hear her say, and when he mutters something about sax lessons, she waves that idea away. "We'll have to focus, Evan, so you might have to make some hard choices." She looks over and notices us standing next to them. "You want to do a good job for the, um, team, right?" she says, giving Evan a not-at-all-subtle head nod toward me. *OMG, Frankie, do you really have no shame?*

Now she turns to face us and seems to realize for the first time that Lillian is there too. Frankie gives her a pathetic attempt at a smile, then looks at me, one raised eyebrow asking, *What's up with this?*

"Hi, Liza, good news. I was just telling Evan here that we could use him on our project. That we'll let him join us, I mean, if he's willing to work hard."

I see where this is going. Take advantage of the poor guy because, for whatever reason, he's decided he likes me. *No way.* Plus, here's Lillian without a partner, and she seems really nice. Nope, I have to put a stop to this.

"Oh wow, that's great," I say, "but it's not necessary. I already asked Lillian." Frankie starts to get a stormy look on her face. She gets like that when things don't go her way, but I'm not going there. There's no way I'm going to spend six weeks "collaborating" with a guy who can't stop staring at me and can barely speak to me without blushing. I turn to Evan, who clearly has no idea what's going on. "You don't mind, right, Evan? I had already asked Lillian, and Frankie didn't know."

Frankie's eyebrow does its thing again. "But, Lize, I already asked Evan." I know Frankie doesn't like to compromise, but I have no idea what she has against Lillian. I try not to look at Lillian because I'm sure she's feeling totally awkward right now. Instead, I turn to Evan with a little wave. "Thanks for understanding."

Evan gives me a goofy smile and backs away, stumbling against a desk as he leaves.

It's so weird! There are plenty of girls in our grade—including Frankie—who have, like, six guys crazy about them at all times. I'm *not* one of them. I have no idea what I did that made Evan decide to like me, but I definitely couldn't deal with a project partner who acts so strange whenever we're within three feet of each other.

Frankie is clearly annoyed at the way this is going. She sits back down at her desk, and Lillian and I grab the two seats next to her, so that we're sitting three across like a game of tic-tac-toe. I'm in the middle, and I look back and forth from one to the other.

"So, now that that's settled," I say, trying to sound positive, "what do you guys think we should do for our project?" All around us, other groups are starting to throw out ideas. I hear Gideon Fuller's booming voice revving up about mapping the waves of immigrants and all the different places they came from. Someone else is talking about researching inventions. Yikes, we have to get on this.

Frankie still won't look at Lillian, and she keeps boring her eyes into me, like she can stare me down and get her way. I decide to show her how great Lillian is going to be as our third project partner.

"Frankie, Lillian was just telling me that her family is from China. Like, *recently*, isn't that cool?"

Frankie keeps looking straight at me. "Totally."

I keep going, because Frankie is being even tougher than usual. Pivoting my head to look at Lillian, I try to tell her with my eyes: *Really, Frankie is the* best *when you get to know her.*

"And she just moved here from San Francisco. . . ."

Frankie glances over at Lillian, then back at me.

"Interesting," she says, in a totally disinterested way.

She takes her eyes off me for a long minute and gives Lillian one of those head-to-toe, up-and-down looks. The three of us don't say anything for a minute. I cannot take this.

I turn back to Lillian.

"Hey, so, I didn't get to ask you. How did you end up at our school?"

Her voice is so low that I have to lean forward to hear it.

"When my parents visited before we moved, they really liked Park Slope. They thought it felt a little bit like our neighborhood in San Francisco." Her eyes dart around the room, before coming back to me.

The rest of us have been at Clinton for a whole year, but I can still remember how I felt on the first day of sixth grade. I was nervous and excited at the same time, like my brain couldn't decide which way to feel so I just felt everything all at once. I'm pretty sure "nervous" would have incinerated "excited" if I'd had to start at a brand-new school all by myself, and after everyone else.

I give Lillian an encouraging grin. "So what do you think?" I ask. "Of Clinton, I mean."

Lillian stares down at her hands. "It's okay," she says, pulling at a hangnail. Then she looks up and shrugs. "Sometimes I just miss my friends."

Frankie and I exchange a look, and I know we're thinking the same thing: If one of us ever moved away from the other, it would be the Worst. Thing. Ever.

Lillian forces a smile. "So," she says in her same quiet voice, "I guess we're supposed to come up with some ideas for the project, right?"

I shift into major student mode and flip a page in my notebook. I notice Frankie picks up her pen too. She rolls her eyes when she catches me smiling at her, but I'm pretty sure she's smiling just a little bit.

"Right," I say, looking from one to the other. "What have we got?"

Before anyone has time to answer, the lights switch on and off again and Mr. McEnroe says it's time to wrap things up. I look down at my blank notebook and know just what Frankie must be thinking: If it were just the two of us, we'd have five pages full of notes and ideas by now. She's right, but it's not my fault Mr. Mac wanted to "stir things up" and make us work in groups of three.

"We should all meet up after school this week to work on the project," I say.

To my surprise—and I'm pretty sure Lillian's, too—Frankie turns to Lillian and flashes her most charming smile. "How about at your house?" she suggests. I stare at her for a split second, and then I realize that Mr. McEnroe has just walked up. She's obviously trying to impress him. He gives her shoulder an absentminded pat before moving on to other groups. Frankie closes her eyes and sighs. She's definitely going to have that T-shirt framed.

# CHAPTER 5
## *Frankie*

Now I know what it means when they say "New World Order."

Ever since Liza sprang this whole Lillian thing on me a few days ago, I've been trying to talk to her about it. I mean, it's not like we don't have other friends, we do; but it's *us*, and then everybody else. At home I'm the only girl in a house full of boys, and practically ever since Ms. Hirshman made us line partners in kindergarten, Liza has been the sister I always wanted. Now, all of a sudden, without consulting me, she brings in the new girl and thinks I should like it?

I've tried to bring it up a million times, but either Liza's running off somewhere or Lillian just happens to be there. Who knew we had so many classes together? And when I text her about it, Liza seems determined to answer as vaguely as possible. Evasion. I get it. Well, two can play that game.

Mr. McEnroe says we have a week to come up with a topic for our project, but I've decided that the sooner we figure it out the better—then we can just divide up the work and do it independently. Or, better yet, Lillian can handle her piece while Liza and I work our magic as a team.

In the meantime, we're all supposed to meet at Lillian's house to brainstorm ideas. I'm on my way to Liza's locker to pick her up, and out of nowhere, Lillian materializes. Of course.

"Hey, Franks!" Liza says, grabbing my arm. "We thought we could all just hop on the train and head over to Lillian's together." Lillian smiles and nods.

*Oh, we did, did we?* I think fast.

"Great idea," I say. "But, Lize, we said we'd water the planters for the Garden Committee, remember? We can't forget to do that." I turn to Lillian. "Why don't you go on ahead and we'll catch up?"

I see Lillian look at Liza, who starts to say something but then changes her mind. "Oh, that's right, sorry. It won't take us long, but if you want to go on home, we can definitely follow."

Lillian nods and gives us her address, then heads down the hall to her locker. She looks back at us once, as if we might have disappeared.

We're not actually signed up for an official watering shift today, but we go through the motions anyway since we have to kill time before heading to Lillian's. We troop down to the janitor's closet near the gym to get enormous watering cans and the wrench to turn on the hose. Mike, the janitor, salutes us when we pass him on the stairs.

Filling up the cans at the spout, Liza watches me, like I'm a time bomb ready to go off.

"Frankie," she says, almost cautiously, as we slosh our way to the front of the building. "Did we really have to do this today? I thought our day was tomorrow."

"No, it's today," I lie. "Or maybe not, I can't remember. But I thought we should just go ahead and do it rather than put it off. It's the responsible thing to do."

Liza takes one of the watering cans and I take the other as we work our way from planter to planter.

"Hmm, and that's Francesca Caputo, always the responsible one, right?"

"Liza, if you have something to say, say it."

"Franks," she says, giving me one of her smiles. Doesn't she get exhausted, being so bright and cheery all the time? "I think you didn't want to walk home with Lillian."

"So sue me if I want to hang out with my best friend for two seconds, is that such a crime?"

Liza drops her almost-empty can and pushes her curls back from her forehead. "No, I guess not. But we're working with Lillian on this, and you need to make more of an effort to be nice. I know you don't really know her—I don't either—but she seemed so lonely during that interview that I just had to ask her to team up with us."

"But that's just it, Liza," I say. "You just went ahead and asked her without even consulting me."

Liza rolls her eyes. "Didn't you ask Evan Jacoby without consulting me?"

She has a point. We round the corner to the last set of planters. There's just enough in the watering cans to dampen the soil, but I don't feel like going all the way back to the faucet. I'm not *that* responsible.

"Hey, that's different," I say. "Evan is really—" I stop because Liza's eyes are pleading.

She puts her hand on my shoulder. "Frankie, it won't kill you to be a little nicer to Lillian. You don't have to be friends, but we're a team for this project and she's going to be great. Better than Evan Jacoby—I promise."

I sigh. "Okay, okay. I'll try. It's just that usually we rock this stuff, and I feel like we're getting off to a bad start. Conner Berman's group is already cutting wood for dioramas, and we don't even have a topic!"

We pick up our empty cans and head back to the closet to put them away, dodging all the stragglers racing out of school who practically mow us down.

"Hey!" I say at the receding backs of a bunch of thick-necked guys who remind me of my brothers. "What are we, invisible? We are trying to walk here!"

Liza laughs and hooks her arm into mine as we head down the hill to the subway station.

"Conner Berman, Franks? I think he's what you

might call OCD, and I don't exactly see us modeling our study habits after his. Does that kid ever eat or drink or sleep or turn on a TV?"

We hop on the train for the short ride to Lillian's. She's right, of course.

"Nah. I know. We just have to rock this project."

Liza laughs and gives me a look. There's no way she suspects I have a crush on Mr. Mac . . . is there? "Sure, Frankie, sure," she says. By the time she stops giggling, we're practically at Lillian's.

# CHAPTER 6
## *Lillian*

As soon as I walk in the door, I hear it: "Shoes off in the house, Lillian!"

This is how my mother greets me every day. This afternoon it's just her voice issuing the warning—the rest of her must be in the kitchen because the smell of garlic and ginger is filling the front hall. The trouble is, since we just moved in a few weeks ago, we haven't put any rugs down yet, and the old wood floors are freezing cold.

"They are off, Mama," I lie, tiptoeing to the stairs so I can run up to my room and grab my slippers. There's no fooling my mother, of course, no matter how often I try.

"I hear the clop, clop, clop like a horse," she says, stepping into the hallway and waving a bamboo spatula at my feet. "Off!"

I do what she says and then dash upstairs for my slippers. Unlike the rest of the house, my room is a mess, but I find the slippers right where I left them this morning, one sticking out from under the comforter and the other in the laundry basket. When we moved, my parents let Katie and me get all new furniture and decorate our bedrooms ourselves. But even though I really like all of my new stuff, nothing about this place feels like "my room" or "my house"—at least not yet.

It's a decent-looking house, I guess, with four floors and gardens in the front and back. And Park Slope seems like an okay neighborhood. But *my* house is back home in San Francisco, with a view of the Golden Gate Bridge and a secret stairway right outside my bedroom leading down to the kitchen. My house is just up the street from my best friend, Sierra, and three blocks away from my cousin Chloe. My house is where I learned to walk and read and where everyone in the neighborhood came over for a big party every Chinese New Year.

Only the smells of our new place remind me of home. As soon as we moved to New York, my mother took Katie and me to Chinatown to find the shops that sell her favorite herbs and spices, lumpy vegetables and dried mushrooms, fish and other things that, trust me, you don't even want to know about. My mother is a biologist—she studies the way mice behave when you interrupt their sleep or blindfold them, that sort of thing—but cooking is her real passion. She's taking a year off from the lab because of the big move, and she can't be happy unless her kitchen is stocked with ingredients and at least two pots are simmering on the stove. The boxes labeled COOKWARE were the first ones to be unpacked when we moved into our new house.

With my feet now cozy in my yellow fuzzy slippers, I grab a pile of paper and some pencils and head downstairs to set up my supplies at the kitchen table. Liza and Frankie are coming over to work on our social studies project, and I want to have everything ready. It'll just be the three of us, but my mother is cooking enough food for the entire seventh grade. Right now there are *xiā jiǎo* (shrimp dumplings) boiling, bean thread noodles sautéing, and some kind of whole fish baking in the oven. I told her not to go overboard, but she couldn't help herself.

"They are your first friends in Brooklyn," she said. "I will not allow them to go home hungry. Besides, food is strength. You will need it for your assignment." Even though my mother has lived in the U.S. for decades, she still believes that the "Chinese way" is the best way, and it's like she has a hard drive in her brain full of old sayings and proverbs for pretty much every situation. There's no arguing with her about food or homework, so I don't even try. I just hope that Liza and Frankie are hungry—and that they like Chinese food.

The doorbell rings and I run to answer it. I'm still not used to the skinny hallway that leads to the front door—you practically have to hold your breath just to squeeze by the stairs.

"Oh my God, what is that smell?" Liza asks as soon as I open the door. "I could smell it halfway down the block!"

"Oh, that's just my mother. She's making us something to eat," I say, cringing. "I hope you're not grossed out."

"Grossed out?" Liza says, closing her eyes and inhaling deeply, like our gym teacher, Tanya, taught us to do in a yoga demo. "Are you kidding? It's like a restaurant in here!" She looks at Frankie and tugs on her sleeve. "Don't you think so, Franks?"

Frankie nods. "Oh yeah, definitely," she says, looking at Liza. She's smiling, but I get the feeling she's being sarcastic.

I close the door and lead them to the kitchen—after they take off their shoes—where my mother has laid out plates for each of us with a little of everything on them. We settle at the table, and she brings us steaming cups of jasmine tea.

"You must be Liza and Frankie," my mother says. "I am Dr. Wong. Lillian has really been looking forward to your visit."

"Ma." I cringe. I cannot believe she just said that. As if they didn't already think I was an enormous dork.

"Did you really make this, Dr. Wong?" Liza asks. She can't take her eyes off the food, so maybe she *didn't* hear my mother make me sound like a total loser.

"This?" my mother says, as if she'd handed us a hunk of Velveeta and a box of saltines. Chinese people are superstitious about accepting compliments, and my mom is a master at pretending to be modest. "Just a little snack. I hope you like fish."

"It looks delicious," Liza says, picking up her chopsticks like a pro and taking a bite. I can tell my mother is impressed that she knows how to use them. "Mmmmm. Oh wow, this is so good."

Frankie obviously doesn't have as much practice and scowls as she stabs at her noodles, unable to grasp any long enough to reach her mouth. Seeing this, my mother immediately grabs a fork from the drawer and places it on the table next to Frankie's plate. Frankie gives her another one of those half smiles. "Thanks."

Frankie's reaction doesn't faze my mother, and she's clearly pleased with the impression she and her spread have made. "I will leave you to your project now, girls," she says. "There's plenty more on the stove if you're hungry. Lillian, don't forget to offer your friends seconds."

Ugh. Did she have to say that? I hardly know Liza

and Frankie, and while I'm dying to make some new friends, I don't want them to think I told my mother we were BFFs or anything.

"Does your mom always cook like this?" Frankie asks after my mom has finally left the room.

"Pretty much," I say with a shrug.

Frankie raises her eyebrow and puts down her fork. Like most of her looks, I'm not sure what it means, but I feel my cheeks starting to burn and I'm pretty sure I'm about to turn as red as the string of chili peppers hanging next to the stove.

"The idea that someone might leave her house hungry is my mother's worst nightmare," I say. "It's really embarrassing."

"Embarrassing?" says Liza. "Um, are you kidding? Your mom is amazing! This is so much better than the Chinese takeout my mom always gets."

"Thanks," I say, thinking about how fun it would be to order takeout of any kind sometime. My mother is a snob when it comes to food, especially

Chinese food. She thinks all of the Chinese restaurants around here are too "Americanized" and won't let us eat at any of them. "Who knows where they get their ingredients?" my mother said with a snooty face the one time I asked. MeiYin Wong definitely does not do takeout.

"You should be grateful your mom can cook like this," Frankie says, poking at a *xiā jiǎo*. "Mine can barely pour cereal."

Liza laughs. "That's true," she says, "but your dad is a great cook. You have nothing to complain about."

"Yeah," says Frankie, "but if I keep eating so much three-alarm chili and four-cheese lasagna, I'm going to end up looking like a five-hundred-pound sumo wrestler." Frankie puffs out her cheeks and puts her arms around her imaginary potbelly, but the real Frankie is anything but fat. She's thin, but not too thin—the kind of girl who looks good in anything she wears. I'm a typical Asian girl, skinny and straight as a twig. If I didn't have long hair, you'd swear I was a boy. My sister, Katie, is fifteen, and she's still shaped just like me (except that she's gorgeous and brilliant and talented and perfect).

Frankie gives up on her dumpling and pushes away her plate. "So," she says, "we should probably start brainstorming ideas for our social studies project, right?" If you really think about it, the word "brainstorming" sounds pretty creepy, but teachers in New York seem to use it as often as my teachers in California did.

While Liza slurps down the last of her noodles, I move my pile of paper to the middle of the table and hand everyone a sharpened pencil.

Frankie puts down the chewed-up pencil stub she was using and dramatically touches the point of the pencil I gave her as if it were the blade of a knife. "Wow, Lillian," she says. "Everything around here is perfect, isn't it?" She makes quotes with her fingers around the word "perfect," and I feel my cheeks start to burn again.

"Seriously," says Liza, smiling as she looks around my mother's spotless, organized kitchen. "Do you think your parents would mind if I moved in?" She's kidding, but in a good way, and I start to relax, even though Frankie rolls her eyes.

Finally, we put our plates in the sink and get down to business, trying to come up with a good idea for our project. Mr. McEnroe says we have to "explore an aspect of immigration"—but which one, and how? We each throw out ideas, but none of them is The One, at least according to Frankie. Liza says maybe we could do an oral history on the journey to America, but who would we interview? The only immigrants we can think of that we could talk to in person are Frankie's grandparents, but she says one set is in Italy taking care of a sick relative, and the other set is too hard to understand. Or my parents, I guess, but there's not much history to record when it comes to their journey.

I suggest that we focus on the lives of immigrant

kids. But Liza says she overheard Stacy Marcus's group talking about doing their project on children, and Frankie thinks it's "unoriginal" to choose the same topic as someone else. She crosses that suggestion off the list right away. Her own idea is to do a photo essay on the kinds of clothes different immigrant groups wore, but then she decides that a project about fashion doesn't feel "brilliant" enough.

After a while our brainstorming feels more like "brain drizzling," and we decide we've worked hard enough for one afternoon. Liza looks out the back door and notices the giant pumpkin growing in our garden, so we all go outside to look at it. Liza says that it's the biggest pumpkin she's ever seen and that if she were me, she couldn't wait to turn it into a jack-o'-lantern. I don't tell her that I've never actually carved a jack-o'-lantern because Halloween is one of the "silly American traditions" my parents don't bother celebrating. Frankie looks bored and gives the pumpkin a little kick, until Liza knocks her foot out of the way.

"I can't take her anywhere," Liza jokes. She's smiling, but I can tell she's squeezing Frankie's hand harder than she has to as she pushes her toward the front door.

After Liza and Frankie leave, I'm in such a good mood that I get started on the rest of my homework without my mother having to bug me about it. So what if we still haven't decided on a topic for our social studies project and Frankie wasn't exactly friendly? Liza is really nice, and for two whole hours I didn't even think about my old school or Sierra and Chloe once, which makes it the best afternoon I've had in Brooklyn so far.

# CHAPTER 7
## *Liza*

When I get off the bus from Lillian's, it's five thirty, which means right now my mom is probably rushing out of her office to pick up my two-year-old brother, Cole, from the day-care center in her building. She's an editor for a parenting magazine, which is kind of funny when you consider how frazzled being a parent makes her. I'm what's known as a "latchkey kid," so I'm pretty much on my own until my mom gets home. Before my parents got divorced and money wasn't so tight, I had a nanny named Sonya who helped take care of me from the time I was three months old until Cole was born and my mom went on maternity leave. Sonya was like part of the family, and I really miss her. She still comes over to visit sometimes, but it's not the same.

I'm still full from the feast Lillian's mom made for us, but as soon as I walk in the door, I open the refrigerator like I always do. Just out of habit. The inside of our fridge is a pitiful sight. Other than juice, milk, and an old bottle of Sprite that went flat sometime in June, there are exactly seven things inside: a bag of baby carrots, applesauce for Cole, a bottle of hot sauce, blueberry jam, two peaches, and a big tub of plain low-fat yogurt that my mom eats with granola every morning.

I close the fridge and pour myself a glass of water from the faucet. Cole's half-empty sippy cup and his cereal bowl with soggy Cheerios from this morning floating in it are still in the sink, so I load them into the dishwasher, which I discover hasn't been run since the weekend. It's like this most of the time these days. My mom is so busy that if we're not close to running out of plates or clean clothes, she decides that the dishes and the laundry can wait. I try to help out as much as I can, but it's so quiet around here in the afternoons that I usually go over to Frankie's, where being alone is basically impossible. Even Lillian's spotless, orderly house felt friendlier to me than our apartment does when it's just me by myself. If it weren't for Cole's blanket crumpled up on the couch and his Thomas trains on the floor near the fireplace, I think even the furniture might get lonely. Mom and Dad were starting to look for a new place—a bigger one—after Cole was born, but then my dad got a job offer in L.A. and, well, the rest is history.

Since we spent the afternoon working on our project—even if we never actually came up with a topic—I plop down on the couch and decide to reward myself with a half hour of TV before starting on the rest of my homework. My favorite show of the moment comes on at five thirty, so I've only missed the beginning. It's a cooking show called *Antonio's Kitchen*, and the host is this really funny guy named Chef Antonio Garcia. Frankie says I'm a cooking show addict, and I guess it's true. I'm totally obsessed with them, and so is my mom. I like *Antonio's Kitchen* best because they tape the show right here in Brooklyn, and sometimes they even show Chef Antonio shopping for ingredients at the same stores my mom and I go to. Used to go to, I mean, before the Big D, a.k.a. my parents' divorce.

Today Chef Antonio is making roast chicken and potatoes, and it looks so good, I can almost smell it through the TV. The whole idea of the show is that you can make really amazing, delicious meals with basic, local ingredients that you can get right in your own neighborhood. Chef Antonio cooks all different types of food, but since he's Cuban, he likes to add a little bit of spice to everything. That's kind of the way my mom cooks too (when she cooks, that is). She's from Atlanta, and she likes her food spicy. No matter how long it is between trips to the grocery store, there's always at least one bottle of hot sauce in the fridge at our own house.

Even though I pigged out at Lillian's, Chef Antonio's chicken is making me hungry. It's almost six, and my mom and Cole will be home soon, so I open our "dinner drawer" and start flipping through the stack of takeout menus. While I'm debating between Indian and Middle Eastern, a commercial at the end of the show catches my attention. *Antonio's Kitchen* is on our local PBS station, so there aren't usually commercials, but this one is an ad for a cooking class with Chef Antonio as the teacher.

"If you love our show," Chef Antonio says as if he's talking directly to me, "then you'll go loco for my live, six-week cooking class right here in our studio!"

I drop the menus on the counter. I would *so* go loco for that class.

"This session's theme is American Cooking 101," Chef tells me. "Over the course of six two-hour classes, we'll explore the vast array of cultures and cooking traditions that make up the melting pot we now think of as distinctly American cuisine. And as always, we'll put the *Antonio's Kitchen* spin on your favorite classic recipes, with fresh seasonal ingredients, a little imagination, and a whole lot of flavor."

Just then I hear a key in the lock and, "Uppy me, Mama, uppy me!" I turn around to see the door swing open with my mom behind it, carrying bags over one arm and trying to pick up cranky Cole with the other. I rush over to take her briefcase from her, along with Cole's Curious George backpack and a bag of apples. My little brother is really sweet most of the time, but when he's tired and hungry, he's like a mini supervillain and it's best to just let my mom deal with him.

"What's for dinner, Lize?" my mom asks as she settles Cole into his high chair and grabs a hot dog from the freezer. Hot dogs are Cole's favorite, so I try not to think about the article we read in health class about all of the disgusting things that are actually in them. At least the ones we have are organic, and to be honest, I like them too. My mom pops Cole's dinner into the microwave and looks up at the TV. Chef Antonio is slicing up his roast chicken while the credits roll on the bottom of the screen. "Mmm, now that looks good," Mom says. "And so does he! Do you think he delivers?"

I laugh, even though I still don't like it when my mom makes comments about men who aren't my dad, and hand her the menus I'd been considering before the commercial distracted me. She spreads them out on the counter and studies them as she washes and peels an apple for Cole. My mom is a master multi-tasker. Seriously, she could teach courses in it. She can bathe Cole, help me with my homework, and polish her own toenails all at the same time.

We agree on Middle Eastern, and I call in our

order while my mom makes sure that at least some of Cole's dinner actually makes it into his mouth. (Don't ask me why, but my brother insists on mashing food into his hair whenever he can—his food, my food, *any* food.) A new show has started on TV, but it's not about cooking, so I turn it off.

"How was your day, Lize?" my mom asks as she scrubs practically Cole's entire head with a baby wipe. "Have you finished your homework?"

Before I can answer either of her questions, she's already halfway to Cole's room to get him ready for bed. I pull my math folder out of my backpack and try to make sense of tonight's worksheet. I've always been good at math, but this year it's pre-algebra and some of the problems just make my brain hurt.

I'm about halfway done when the doorbell rings, and suddenly, there's Cole, running down the hallway in his diaper yelling, "Dinner! Dinner!" He's right this time, but the really funny thing is that he says that every time the doorbell rings, no matter what time of day it is. Sometimes Frankie picks me up on the way to school in the morning, and even when she rings the bell at seven forty-five a.m., Cole comes racing to the door, fully expecting to see the deliveryman waiting there with a big white bag.

My mom comes in, scoops up Cole, and tosses her purse at me. I pay the delivery guy and start setting out our food on the coffee table while Mom gets Cole settled in his crib and reads him a story. Our apartment does have an actual dining table, but we have this nightly ritual where we watch the cooking channel together and eat our dinner in front of the TV. I know, I know, kids do better in school and don't end up doing drugs when families sit down at the table for dinner. But so far I've never gotten below a B and I don't even know anyone who does drugs, so I don't think our mother-daughter TV dinners are going to mess me up too much.

By the time my mom has finished reading to Cole, I've arranged our meals on our plates like they do in food magazines and I've poured us both iced tea in my favorite polka-dot glasses. When I turn on the TV, it's still on PBS and that same commercial for Chef Antonio's cooking class comes on again. I watch the ad a second time while my mom changes into sweatpants—she says whoever invented work clothes must have hated being comfortable.

Chef Antonio looks me in the eye and tells me every class will feel like a fiesta. I've never been to a fiesta, but even the word sounds fun. My mom plops herself down on the couch and glances at the TV. "A cooking class, huh? I used to love those," she says as she unwraps the napkin around her plastic silverware. "But seriously, who has the time?" She digs in to her takeout shish kebab and takes a long sip of iced tea.

And just like that, I have an idea. An absolutely amazing, totally brilliant idea. I can't wait to tell Frankie about it.

# CHAPTER 8
## *Frankie*

My house is like Cirque du Soleil minus the talent and the really cool costumes. Four kids, two working parents, and one small, but very sloppy, slightly stinky dog create a recipe for major chaos. Of course I missed Liza's text last night and didn't see it until this morning. Why? Because my little brother Nicky swiped my phone and hid it in a tissue box in my room—his idea of a hilarious joke—where I never would have looked for it if I hadn't just sneezed myself awake.

Here's what Liza's text said: *I have a BIG idea. Call me.*

Since I didn't read it until just now, I obviously didn't call Liza last night. Big idea? For what? Our project? It sounds even bigger than that.

I don't have time to think about it because Nicky runs in carrying a bottle of maple syrup and yelling something about waffles. As usual, Rocco is trotting along behind him, panting and drooling. Have I mentioned that it's 6:25 a.m.?

"Me and Rocco are hungry, Frankie." Nicky's piercing voice drills directly into my ear and his dark curls tickle my cheek. "We want waffles! Where's Pop?"

Don't ask me why Nicky calls my dad "Pop." It started when he was a baby and liked the Dr. Seuss book *Hop on Pop*, and it stuck. The rest of us call him "Dad," although my older brothers, Leo and Joey (a.k.a. The Goons), call basically everyone "Yo."

"Dad's sleeping," I say. "You and Rocco will have to wait till later."

My dad has been a firefighter for more than twenty years, which means he almost never has to work the night shift anymore. But everyone in his squad has to do an overnight at least sometimes, and last night was Dad's turn. On mornings like this he comes home around five and locks himself in the guest room in the basement (which is really more like the ground floor in old brownstone houses like ours). No one's supposed to bother him until after school, but Nicky usually forgets, so even though I'm totally annoyed that he's in my face, it's a good thing he came to bug me instead of Dad.

"I need waffles now, Frankie. We're starving."

"Ask Mom," I say, burrowing back into my pillow. "And both of you get your smelly paws off my bed."

"No way!" Nicky shrieks, plopping himself down next to me on my bed. "Mom stinks at waffles. Remember before?"

Unfortunately, I do. The last time my mom tried to make waffles, she ended up melting all the kitchen tools. It wasn't totally her fault—the jar of utensils fell on the open waffle iron after she'd plugged it in. But she was so focused on trying to "gently fold egg whites" into the lumpy batter that she didn't notice all the melting spatulas and spoons. How she missed the disgusting smell, I have no idea, but by the time she turned to pour the batter on the machine, the smoke alarm had gone off and we ended up having to leave the windows open for two days. In February.

"How about cereal?" I say. "Mom can make that."

"Waffles, Frankie, waffles!" hollers Nicky, who's now jumping up and down on my bed.

"Aaargh!" I scream, pulling my pillow over my head. "Leave me alone!"

Of course, Nicky ignores me. "Waffles! Waffles! Waffles!" he yells, over and over, still jumping.

All the hollering gets Rocco excited, and he starts barking like crazy. That wakes up The Goons, who share a giant room right next to mine. They bang on the wall with their big meaty fists and yell things like, "Shut up or I'll kill you!" It's a good thing we don't live in an apartment like Liza does, or our neighbors would totally have the police on speed dial.

Finally, Mom comes in to see what all the insanity is about. I don't know if Nicky notices her, but he keeps right on jumping and screaming like a maniac at the top of his lungs. My mom is dark-haired, and pretty, in a distracted sort of way, but right now she looks sleep-deprived and more than a bit crabby.

"Nicky!" my mom tries to yell above my brother's loud, annoying waffle chant. "Stop that jumping and use your inside voice immediately!"

My mom teaches second grade, and when she gets mad, she goes into teacher mode and says things like, "Use your inside voice" and "Keep your hands on your own body." Sometimes she even claps—one, two, one-two-three—to get us to calm down. Joey, Leo, and I have to force ourselves not to crack up when she does it, but since Nicky's in second grade, it usually works on him.

Nicky stops jumping on my bed, but instead of sitting down or stepping off, he leaps into the air and lands right on top of Mom. She obviously wasn't expecting her seven-year-old son to come flying into her arms, so the two of them crash onto the floor, freaking out Rocco and making him bark even louder. I just want to roll over in disgust and go back to bed, but that is *so* not happening.

The crash is enough to get The Goons out of bed, and they burst through the door demanding to know what *I* think *I'm* doing waking them up at this hour. When they stomp into my room, The Goons are like loud, massive, hairy boy monsters with major B.O. They are *so* annoying. They finally notice Mom thrashing around on the floor trying to get Nicky off her as he squeals like a hyena, but all they do is snort with laughter. They don't even bother to give her a hand.

As usual, it's my job to come to the rescue, and I'm

on my way to help my mom up when I feel the vibrations of slow, heavy footsteps on the stairs. Everyone else must have felt them too, because we all freeze, and suddenly, everyone is silent, even Rocco, who looks from one of us to the other wondering what's up.

*Who's* up is the real question, and the answer is my dad. He's an easygoing, fun-loving guy most of the time, but when he's woken up early after a night on duty, watch out. At six foot two and two hundred pounds, Dad's a big guy. He spends his days saving people's lives and would never hurt a fly, but he can be seriously scary when he's mad.

We all stare silently as my dad enters my room, looking like Bigfoot after a rough night in the forest. It's gotten really crowded in here with all of us squeezed into this microscopic space, and with Dad's arrival, the atmosphere becomes tense. His large hazel eyes are usually welcoming, but right now they're all bloodshot and puffy. He glares at each of us with a look that says, *This had better be good,* until his gaze lands on Mom on the floor, still stuck under Nicky, who, for some reason known only to his bizarre seven-year-old brain, has not budged from on top of her.

Then something completely weird and unexpected happens: Like one of The Goons, my dad bursts into hysterics, barely able to control himself long enough to help my mom off the floor. Of course, Nicky, Leo, and Joey join in too, and Rocco starts his crazy barking again. Everyone is laughing (and barking) like total nerds, except for Mom and me.

My mom straightens the giant T-shirt that's her version of a nightgown and smoothes her hair as she stands up. She still has major bed head, but this definitely isn't the time to mention it.

"So," she says, and the boys and Dad all try to control their laughter, "if you are all *quite* finished . . . do you still want waffles, Nicky? Who else wants breakfast?" She looks at us expectantly as we all exchange looks that say, *Oh no!*

Dad puts his arm around Mom's shoulders and gives them a squeeze. "I'll take care of breakfast, honey," he says. "Why don't you go and take a nice, long shower?"

"Come on," my mom says, shrugging off his arm. "I can make breakfast. Right, guys?"

I manage to hold in a giggle, but The Goons just crack up again.

"Ma," Leo croaks—he's fifteen, so his voice is changing, and everything he says sounds like it's coming from the bullfrog pond at the children's zoo— "leave it to Dad. You dumped the spaghetti all over your foot last night when you were trying to drain it, remember? We had to keep it in a tub of ice water all night and eat frozen pizza. There wasn't even enough for all of us, and I think I ate a whole box of cereal, too."

Who is he kidding? He *always* eats whole boxes of cereal.

My dad looks alarmed. "Hon, your foot? I knew I should have heated up something for you guys before

I headed out to my shift." Mom rolls her eyes and waves him away impatiently.

"No way Mom's cooking!" Nicky yells. "You burn everything!"

"Or undercook it," adds Joey. "Remember that French toast she made on your birthday, Nicky? You stuck your fork in and the eggs oozed out all over your plate. Like alien guts!" Joey runs his hands all over Nicky's face like slimy egg yolks, which makes the little squirt scream. Again. I want them out of my room. Like, now.

"Her oatmeal's not bad," Leo squawks. "You know, if you like your oatmeal cold and crunchy."

Mom puts her hand on her hip. "Ha-ha. Very funny," she says. "You know that only happened once."

We all look at her like she's nuts.

"Okay, maybe twice. But I'm much better at it now and you know it."

I try to think of something supportive—but not

*too* supportive—to say, but before I have the chance, Joey pushes by me on his way to the door. "Sorry, Ma," he says, patting her head like she's a little girl, "but your cooking is the worst. Nice bed head, though."

My dad gives Joey a smack on his butt as he heads toward the bathroom. "Hey, don't talk to your mother like that!" Dad calls after him, but you can tell from his eyes that his heart isn't in it. I'm pretty sure it's taking all of his strength to keep from laughing again.

"Mom can't cook," Nicky says matter-of-factly, handing my dad the maple syrup and dragging him out toward the stairs. "I want Pop's waffles!"

"Okay, then," says Dad. "Waffles it is! Get your-selves dressed and meet me in the kitchen in fifteen."

Everyone leaves my room at last, except for my mom, who's giving me a look. "Even you, Frankie?" she says. "It's just us two girls around here. We're sup-posed to stick up for each other."

"Sorry, Mom." I shrug. "I know you really like to cook in theory, but maybe . . . well, maybe you just need more practice."

I feel kind of bad for her, so in a move that's totally out of character for me, I give my mom a kiss on the cheek. Then I squeeze past her through the door in search of an empty bathroom. With six people sharing only two full bathrooms, showering is a competitive sport in our house.

"How am I supposed to get any practice," my mom calls after me, "if no one around here ever lets me cook?"

It's not until the middle of my shower, while I'm making a tower of my suds-filled hair, that I remember Liza's text about her big idea. Suddenly, I can't wait to get to first period, even though it's math. I make a mental note to bring Liza some of my dad's waffles, if there are any left over.

# CHAPTER 9
## *Lillian*

If I were a middle-school principal, I would make a rule against first-period math class. Seriously, whose brain can handle something as totally confusing as pre-algebra at eight fifteen? Not mine, although there isn't actually any time of day when pre-alg makes much sense to me. Unlike my sister, Katie, I've never been very good at math. You know that stereotype about all Asians being math whizzes? Well, I'm living proof that it's definitely *not* true. My best subjects are creative writing and art, which isn't terribly impressive to my scientist parents or Katie, the junior genius.

This morning I drag myself to the overly bright math classroom early to spend a few extra minutes going over the homework sheet. Liza must have had the same idea, because she's already there huddled over the handout when I walk in. Even though Liza was just at my house yesterday, we're not technically friends (yet), and I feel weird taking the seat right next to her. I decide to sit down behind her instead.

"Hi," I say as I walk past Liza's desk.

She looks up. "Hey!" she says. "Did you finish the assignment? I can't believe how hard it was."

I take out my half-done homework. "Not exactly. I'm sort of mathematically challenged."

"Yeah," says Liza, "I think I am too."

This is totally untrue. Liza is one of the best students in the class and I bet she got every problem on the homework right. Unlike my sheet, which is covered in scratch-out and eraser marks, Liza's still looks fresh from the printer, with a neatly written answer in every blank.

It dawns on me that Ms. Hernandez is not at her desk at the front of the room, which is definitely unusual. "Do you think we have a substitute?" I ask.

Liza's eyes widen. "Oh, man," she says. "That would be too good to be true."

For a minute it looks like Liza is right as the door to the classroom begins to open. But instead of Ms. Hernandez, it's Frankie, carrying a big Tupperware container and a bottle of maple syrup.

"There you are!" she says to Liza. "I've been standing at your locker for, like, ten years." Frankie plops the container and syrup on Liza's desk and dumps the rest of her stuff on the next seat over.

"Try ten minutes," Liza says with laugh. She eagerly examines the Tupperware that has suddenly appeared in front of her. "What the heck is this?"

"Leftovers from breakfast at my house," Frankie says. "My dad's waffles. Luckily, The Goons had morning track practice, or there wouldn't have been any left."

"Yum," says Liza, opening the container. "But how am I supposed to eat them?"

Frankie points at Liza's desk. "With a pencil, Einstein, what do you think?"

Liza raises her eyebrows and looks at me. I don't know Frankie well enough yet to tell if she's joking, so I just give a little shrug.

"Kidding!" Frankie laughs. She digs into her bag and pulls out a fork. "Here. You might want to wipe it off before you use it—Nicky's been known to hide his 'discoveries' in my backpack."

"Wow, thanks," Liza says. She takes the fork from Frankie and digs into the waffles. After a bite or two she turns to me. "You've gotta try these, Lillian. Frankie's dad's waffles are practically famous."

Frankie looks up and seems to notice me for the

first time since she walked in. "Oh hi, Lillian. Yeah, sure, have a bite."

I stab a little pile of waffles and try to look normal as I stuff the whole forkful in my mouth. *Wow.* I close my eyes and savor its sweet deliciousness.

"Yum," I say. "I can see why these are famous."

Frankie rolls her eyes. "They're only famous in her mind." She turns back to Liza. "Speaking of your mind, what's this 'big idea'?" she asks, making air quotes when she says it. "I can't take the suspense one second longer!"

Liza puts down her fork and takes her time chewing her last bite.

"C'mon," Frankie says. "Swallow already!"

Liza takes a long sip from her water bottle to wash down the waffles. I can tell she's enjoying making Frankie wait for whatever it is she's going to tell her. I know it's none of my business, but now I'm really curious about Liza's big idea too.

"So," Liza leans in toward Frankie, "you know

how I'm sort of obsessed with that cooking show on Channel 16?"

"You mean the one with the really cute Spanish chef?" asks Frankie.

"Yeah, yeah. *Antonio's Kitchen*," says Liza. "And Spanish people are from Spain, brainiac. Chef Antonio is Cuban."

I hold in a giggle because I don't want Liza and Frankie to think I'm eavesdropping. Even though I sort of am.

"Anyway . . . ," says Frankie.

"So, anyway," Liza continues, "I was watching it last night after I got home, and during the show an ad came on for an *Antonio's Kitchen* cooking class— right here in Brooklyn."

Frankie nods her head but looks as though she's still not sure what Liza is getting at.

"The class is called American Cooking 101," says Liza, "and it's about how most of the stuff we eat in the United States actually came from other places.

Like, when it comes to food, America really is a giant melting pot."

Frankie looks disappointed. "So your big idea is that you're going to take a cooking class with your celebrity chef crush?"

Liza shakes her head. "Uh-uh," she says, and then smiles like she's about to give Frankie a present. "My big idea is that *we* are going to take a cooking class with my celebrity chef crush." When she says "we," Liza draws a line in the air between herself and Frankie and then—I can hardly believe it—turns around and continues the invisible line until she's pointing directly at me.

Did Liza actually just include *me* in this big plan? I blush and try to act like I've been concentrating on my math sheet rather than their conversation.

"Um, did you say something?" I ask, hoping I don't sound as excited as I feel.

Frankie looks from Liza to me and then back again, as if to say, *Her?*

"Guys," Liza says, jumping up from her chair, "my big idea is for our project! The class is about all the different kinds of foods that make up American cooking. And guess who brought them here? Immigrants! Every group of immigrants had to eat, right? And they each brought their own style of cooking with them. So we'll take the class and then use what we learn to do a project about immigration and food!"

Liza plops back into her seat, as if explaining her big idea to us wore her out.

Frankie scrunches up her forehead and straddles her chair. If ever there was a look that said, *I'm thinking,* this is it.

Liza raises her eyebrows at us. "So?"

"Interesting," says Frankie. "Not exactly what I was expecting, but definitely interesting."

"Interesting good or interesting bad?" Liza asks.

"I think it's a great idea!" I practically shout, as if we were talking about a trip to Six Flags instead of a school project. Since my mom refuses to let anyone touch her precious pots and pans, I have basically zero cooking experience. But taking a class with Liza and Frankie is guaranteed to be more fun than anything else I could be doing instead. I have exactly nothing planned for the next six years.

Liza seems pleased with my gung-ho response, but Frankie keeps talking to Liza as if I'm not sitting two feet away from her. "Well," she says, "it does work pretty perfectly with the assignment."

"And," says Liza, like she's about to plop the cherry on top of an ice-cream sundae, "you know Mr. McEnroe is a major foodie, so our topic would definitely impress him, don't you think?"

Frankie's eyes get really wide and practically sparkle. "Oh, Lize, that's so true! You're a total genius!" Then she turns to me and the sparkle fades. "But we don't *all* need to take the class, do we? I mean, can't whoever takes the class just tell whoever doesn't all about it? I mean, it doesn't seem like everyone needs to do everything. . . ."

The way she says "whoever" makes it super clear that "whoever" should take the class is the two of them and "whoever" shouldn't is me. I look down at the floor, my cheeks burning again, but in a totally different way.

Liza picks up the fork from her waffles and pokes Frankie in the hand with it. I can't help hoping it hurts just a little. "Franks," she sighs, "this is a team project, remember?"

"Ouch!" Frankie yelps, pulling her hand away. "Okay, okay." She glances at me and flashes that half smile I'm getting used to. "It'll be fun," she mumbles under her breath.

"Okay!" says Liza, clapping her hands. "We're all in. I'll send you a link to the class after school so we can all register tonight."

"How much does it cost, by the way?" Frankie asks. "You know how my mom and dad are about spending money on 'extras.' Have you asked your mom yet?"

Liza shakes her head. "Not yet. But I looked it up and it's not that much. I can use that money my nana sent me for my birthday, and aren't you still hoarding your Christmas stash from last year?"

"I wasn't exactly planning to use that for a cooking class," Frankie says. "But since it's for our brilliant project, I guess it's worth it."

Liza turns to me. "How about you, Lillian?" she asks. "Do you have anything saved up?"

Before I have a chance to answer, someone in the back of the room groans, and we all turn around to see Ms. Hernandez rush into the room, apologizing for being late. *Phew.* Even though it's actually her and not a sub, I'm glad I don't have to explain that while money would be no problem for me—our relatives all gave Katie and me a big stack of lucky red envelopes full of cash at our good-bye party, and so far I've had nothing to spend it on— convincing my mother to let me take the class is going to be its own kind of project. I decide to use the next forty-five minutes to come up with a plan while Ms. H. drones on about x + y = zzzzzzzz. If I have to put my brain into overdrive during first period, at least today I have something interesting to think about.

# CHAPTER 10
## *Liza*

On the wall above the nurse's desk in the infirmary at school, there's this really goofy poster with ballerinas on it and some corny saying like, *If you can imagine it, you can be it. If you can dream it, you can achieve it.* I'm thinking about that poster right now because I'm about to tell my mom about my big idea, and I need all the wisdom I can get.

Why am I looking to dorky posters for inspiration just to ask my mom if I can take a cooking class that she doesn't even have to pay for? Well, there's kind of a "part two" to my plan that I didn't mention to Frankie or Lillian. The thing is, the class is really for adults—you have to be over eighteen to register. But I called the cooking school, and the receptionist said that as long as one adult signs up to take it with us, Frankie, Lillian, and I are in. My mom used to love to cook. But she never has time anymore. She never has time to do *anything* anymore, except work and take care of Cole. If I can convince her to be our "one adult," maybe she'll start acting like her old self again, even if it's just for two hours a week. That would be the best big idea ever.

I bring up my plan after dinner while Mom's braiding my hair, which is usually when she wants to have "girl talk." My hair is crazy curly, but it's softer and finer than hers, which makes it easier to braid. I'm not into braids all over my head or anything, but a couple of really skinny ones on each side with the rest of my hair hanging loose looks okay and keeps the wild "corkscrews" (that's what my mom calls them) out of my eyes.

When she's braiding, my mom gets into a rhythm that she says is relaxing. That's when she starts asking me questions about my friends and whether I like any boys. Most of my friends hate talking about that stuff with their parents, but my mom and I have always been close, so I don't really mind. However, when it comes to boys, there's never much to tell.

As soon as Mom gets into her braiding groove, I decide the time to drop the idea of Chef Antonio's cooking class on her is now or never.

"Hey, Mom, guess what?" I say in a way that I hope sounds casual yet perky.

"I don't know, honey," she says in that voice she uses when she's in the zone. "Hand me a rubber band and tell me *what.*"

"Well, we came up with a plan for our social studies project," I say.

"That's great, Lize," she mumbles, the rubber

band clenched between her teeth. "So what is it?"

"You know that cooking show I always watch, *Antonio's Kitchen*? Well, Antonio—he's the chef—is teaching a class right here in Brooklyn. It's around the corner from your coffee place, on Atlantic Avenue. We saw the commercial, remember?"

"Uh-huh."

While she yanks at my curls, I tell my mom about American Cooking 101 and how it fits in perfectly with our immigration project. I get so into explaining the idea that I start to turn my head while my mom is braiding, which is never a good idea. She holds the braid tight and gently turns my head so I'm facing forward again.

"So," I go on, reminding myself to talk with my mouth, not my head, "Frankie and our third partner, Lillian—she's new—both think taking the class and doing our project on immigration and food is a great idea. We're even going to make something from the recipes we learn in the class for our presentation—like little replicas for the Immigration Museum that Mr. McEnroe is putting together."

"Wow," Mom says. "Sounds ambitious. But what else is new? Frankie and Lillian are right—it is a great idea for a project, Lize. Do you need me to help you register? How much is it?"

"Well," I say, step one of my mission accomplished, "actually, we're not technically allowed to register unless an adult takes the class with us. So I was thinking you could sign yourself up too."

My mom stops braiding and laughs. Not a good sign. "Oh, you were, huh?"

I spin around to face her, summoning all of my poster wisdom. "You said you used to love taking cooking classes," I remind her. "And it's for my school project, so it'll be like you're helping me with my homework, which you always say you wish you had more time to do."

My mom shakes her head, even though she's smiling. "You've got it all figured out, don't you?"

"All you have to do is sign us up," I say, giving her my best puppy-dog eyes. "I can use my birthday money to pay for it."

Mom turns me around again and starts on the last braid. "Hang on to your birthday money for a minute," she says, in a voice that worries me just a little bit. "I love your enthusiasm, sweetheart, and I love the idea that my twelve-year-old daughter actually wants to spend time with me in public even more."

Uh-oh, there's only one word that comes after a sentence like that.

"But," she says (and that's the one), "you share me with a rambunctious little guy named Cole. Remember him? Curly hair, messy face, about this tall?" She holds her hand up about a foot higher than the coffee table.

I sigh. "Mom, I haven't forgotten about Cole."

"So where exactly does he fit into your grand scheme?" she asks.

"What do you mean?"

My mom ties off my last braid, smoothes the back of my hair, and sits down to face me. "I mean, what do you propose we do with him while we're at cooking class every Saturday? I'm guessing he's too young to sign up with us, since he can't even reach the stove."

"Couldn't you get a babysitter for him?" I suggest. "The class is only for a couple of hours, and it's right at nap time too."

My mom takes my chin in her hand and smiles at me in that "I feel sorry for you" sort of way. "Honey, Cole is at day care for nine hours a day, five days a week," she says. "If I leave him with a babysitter every Saturday afternoon, he's going to start thinking I'm his personal assistant instead of his mommy."

I let my shoulders droop. "But what about me? Don't I get to hang out with you too?"

"Of course you do, Sweet Potato," Mom says. "That's why the weekends are special. They're for family time, when all three of us can hang out together."

I used to love it when my mom called me "Sweet

Potato." It's kind of a funny nickname, I know, but it reminds me of that warm and delicious feeling you get when you walk into the kitchen and smell a freshly baked sweet potato pie. This time, though, all I can picture is a lumpy old root sitting in the dark at the bottom of the vegetable bin.

"It's just a couple of hours, Mom." I sigh. "And it's only for six weeks. I'm pretty sure Cole will survive." I look up at her. "Besides, you do Rock Band Baby just with him. I've never complained about that, have I?"

This time it's my mom who rolls her eyes. "Liza, Rock Band Baby starts at nine o'clock on Saturday mornings," she says. "You're still asleep!"

"Just like Cole will be practically the entire time we're at cooking class," I say back. *So there!*

"You've got an answer for everything, don't you, Liza Louise?" Mom says. She's shaking her head, but she can't help smiling.

Hopeful, I shrug and smile too. "I'm waiting for a 'yes' from you, Jacqueline Dawn."

My mom perfects my braids in some microscopic way and tucks them behind my ears. "Well, you're going to have to settle for an 'I'll think about it' for now, okay?"

I crumple, as if I have appendicitis or I've just been shot or something. "Come on, Mommy, really? Can't you just say yes?" I beg. "Frankie, Lillian, and I can't sign up without you."

"What about Theresa or Joe?" she asks. "Or Lillian's parents? I appreciate that you're asking me to take the class with you girls, but if you need an answer right away, you might want to think about asking one of them."

My mom touches my cheek and gets up to put away the combs and rubber bands. I pick up the hand mirror lying on the coffee table and stare into my own disappointed eyes. I wonder what Frankie and Lillian will say when I tell them that we need an adult to take Chef Antonio's class with us and that it doesn't look like it's going to be my mom. Even if one of their parents agrees to do it, it won't be the same. Getting my mom to remember how much she loves cooking was the whole reason I came up with the plan in the first place. I guess my big idea was really just a Big Dumb Idea.

# CHAPTER 11
## *Frankie*

I have no idea what's up with Liza these days, but she's acting really weird. First she insists on including Lillian in everything we do, and then it turns out she left out a pretty crucial bit of info about her big idea: We can't actually take the cooking class unless an adult signs up with us. Liza sent me this text about how she really wants her mom to do the class, but Cole is ruining everything, as usual. Liza is an amazing big sister and way nicer to Cole than I am to

Nicky—most of the time. But whenever something doesn't go her way, she blames it on the poor little guy, as if being born right before their parents' marriage went down the toilet was all his idea.

Anyway, now Liza wants *me* to ask one of my parents to take the class with us, since we've already started working on our project proposal for Mr. Mac, and the cooking class is a big part of it. Actually, I think she asked Lillian to try too, but even after meeting her mom only once, I know that is *not* going to happen. No way.

Now, my dad is the obvious choice, right? He's practically a chef himself. The problem is, he's on call with his fire company every other Saturday and never knows when he might have to drop everything for an emergency. When I was younger, I used to keep a list of all of the birthday parties, soccer games, and dance recitals my dad missed because he was on duty or on call. I understood that, for him, "going to work" meant putting out fires and saving people's lives, but

I couldn't help wishing he were with me on those big days. By now I'm used to Dad rushing off to the firehouse in the middle of grilling steaks or watching one of The Goons' basketball games, so I don't think he's the kind of reliable adult Chef Antonio is expecting to keep an eye on us during cooking class. Which leaves me with no choice but to ask the one person in our family responsible for the most kitchen disasters: my mom.

Taking a daily walk is one of the few things my mom makes time to do for herself. Early in the morning, when she gets home from work, after dinner . . . she may not do it at the same time every day (that would be impossible in our house), but she does it every day. "If I miss a day of walking, I'll lose my mind," she always says—which is probably true, considering the constant chaos around here.

By "taking a walk," I don't mean going out for a leisurely stroll around the block—I mean a five-mile power walk at a pace even my dad can't keep up with.

Before she messed up her back carrying four kids all over Brooklyn, my mom was a runner. She says walking doesn't feel like exercise the way running did, but whenever I go with her I end up huffing and puffing and sweating like one of The Goons. I don't tag along with her much. But she likes to have company, so my brilliant plan is to bring up the cooking class during a walk. That way, if she gets annoyed, she'll be too winded to do a whole lot of yelling.

As we're getting ready to leave, Nicky is playing with his LEGOS and my older brothers are watching some extreme sports show with their super-cute friend James (who, sadly, is also super dumb). Rocco looks up at my mom and me with his bug eyes and pushed-in nose, his tongue sticking out of the side of his mouth like it always does. He bark-snorts at us, begging us to bring him along, but you can't take a pug on a power walk—they get overheated and can't breathe. Poor Rocco, he should have been born a golden retriever.

My mom and I do some stretches and then head out toward the river, past a row of little shops I love that sell the kind of things you take out of the bag, put on your dresser, look at for a few days, and then forget about until your mom bugs you to dust them. "Tchotchkes," Liza calls them when she's doing her impression of Nana, her grandmother on her dad's side.

We pass the little farm that used to be a parking lot and now grows all kinds of vegetables right here in the middle of the city. Sometimes in the summer we come after camp or on the weekends to help pick buckets of green beans or tomatoes or whatever's ripe. Some college kids are putting signs up around the farm announcing the fall Harvest Festival, and there are loads of pumpkins on the vines that look ready to be picked. My mom points to one of the signs and reminds me that if we bring Nicky to the festival again this year, we'll have to make sure he doesn't terrorize the chickens like he did last time. I decide it's the perfect moment to bring up our big idea.

"Speaking of harvesting," I say (I don't usually say things like "speaking of," but I like the way it sounds—I'll have to remember to try it next time I talk to Mr. McEnroe), "there's a cooking class Liza and this new girl Lillian and I want to take for our social studies project. You don't mind if I sign up, do you?"

My mom slows down a little and looks kind of baffled, but confusion is a pretty normal state for her. "I'm not sure I get the connection, Francesca. A cooking class, for a social studies project? And how much is it, anyway?"

"Well," I say, grateful for the slightly more relaxed pace and a chance to catch my breath, "Liza saw a commercial for this class with that really cute chef from the cooking show she's addicted to, and the theme is American cooking, which works perfectly with our unit on immigration. Get it?"

"*Bella*," my mom says, picking up the pace again now that we are close to the path along the river, "I've got four kids' schedules clogging up my brain. You're going to have to connect the dots for me a little bit here."

Between huffs and puffs, dodging runners and cyclists and strollers, I tell my mom the whole story of how the big idea was born and how it turned into our project for Mr. McEnroe. I leave out the part about us needing her to take the class too—first things first.

We stop for a minute when we reach the water and watch the Staten Island Ferry chug by.

"Get it?" I ask, wishing I'd remembered to bring a water bottle.

"I think so. But you still haven't told me how much it costs."

I tell her my Christmas money should cover it. She looks relieved and kicks into high gear again.

"In that case, I see no reason why you shouldn't take the class, Frankie," she says. "It sounds like fun."

Bingo. "Really?" I say, doing my best to keep pace. "That's great, Mom, because, actually, we kind of need you to take it too."

My mom's baffled look returns. "Excuse me?"

The sun gleams through the Statue of Liberty's crown as I explain how Liza thought her mom would take the class with us, only she forgot about Cole.

Without breaking her stride, my mom wipes the sweat off her forehead with the back of her hand and turns to me. "But why me? We all know the kitchen is your dad's domain."

I go for the big guns. "True. But don't you want to show Dad and the boys that you're not the nightmare in the kitchen that they think you are?"

Suddenly, my mom stops walking, which is definitely not typical Theresa Caputo. "Francesca," she says, "I may not be Julia Child, but I don't think I'm a 'nightmare in the kitchen,' either."

When I don't say anything, she pauses. "Am I?"

If anyone's mom needs a cooking class, it's mine.

The funny thing—in a pathetic sort of way—is that she doesn't think so. I decide the situation calls for some tough love.

"Mom," I say, "you burn everything from toast to chicken wings. Your hot dogs explode, your cake batters are runny, your quesadillas are like rubber, and you've dumped hot pasta water on your foot twice in recent memory. And let's not even talk about that thing with the omelet, okay? Don't you think you could use some professional help?"

My mom sighs and plops down hard on someone else's stoop, even though she hates it when people we don't know hang out on ours.

"Okay, so maybe I am a 'nightmare' when it comes to cooking," she says. "I still like to try. But honestly, sweetie, I love that your dad is the master chef in our family. I feel lucky compared to a lot of moms I know. I don't need to take a class to try to cook as well as he can. I'm happy to let him be King of the Kitchen."

"But, Mom," I plead, "we can't take the class

without an adult, and Dad's on call on Saturdays. It's too late to come up with another project idea, and anyway, this one's really good—Mr. McEnroe's totally going to love it."

My mom looks at me as if everything suddenly makes sense. "Ah-ha! Now the truth comes out: You need me."

I shove her a little with my shoulder. "Come on, Mom, imagine Dad's and the boys' faces when you suddenly whip up a delicious dinner—without anything melting or exploding. They'll be blown away. *And* they won't be able to make fun of your cooking . . . um . . . skills anymore."

My mom considers this and then checks the time on her phone. "Let's walk and talk," she says, hopping up from the stoop.

I follow, a few paces behind, as usual. When I finally catch up, I tug on her sleeve like a little kid begging for another quarter for the gumball machine. "Oh, please, Mommy, we've got to do it!"

"Frankie, you crack me up, you know that?" My mom laughs. Then she speeds up for the last few blocks of the walk home.

When I get there, the door to our house is open, but my mother's still standing on the top step just staring inside. I slide past her and step into one of the most massive messes I've ever seen—and trust me, I've seen a lot. Our house isn't filled with antiques or anything, but we do have some nice furniture that my grandmother gave us when she sold her brownstone and moved into an apartment building. Apparently, Nicky and The Goons decided it would be a good idea to transform the living and dining rooms into an indoor skate park by turning the furniture into ramps and half-pipes. Every chair, table, and sofa has been tipped upside down, or at least on its side. Nicky's entire collection of LEGOs is spilled out all over the carpet to make a "hazard area" that the three of them are trying to avoid as they "skateboard" in their socks and crash into the couch cushions like total dweebs.

I hear what sounds like a cross between a whimper and a growl and kneel down to peek under an overturned side chair. Of course it's Rocco, who clearly can't decide whether to defend his turf or run for his life and has chosen to hide out under his favorite chair instead. I feel a hand on my shoulder and look up. My mom doesn't look angry, upset, or even annoyed, and I decide she must be in shock. "Frankie?" she says.

"Yeah, Mom?" I reply, standing up.

"When did you say that cooking class starts?"

I smile, crossing my fingers on both hands. "Saturday."

Without saying a word to my brothers, my mom puts her arm around my shoulder, grabs her purse, and leads me out of the house. She doesn't look back or even bother to close the door. "I'm in," she says. "Let's go over to that studio and sign ourselves up."

# CHAPTER 12

## *Lillian*

My mother is an ox. Not literally, of course (although she does look a whole lot like one when she's mad). I mean she was born in the Year of the Ox. According to the Chinese zodiac, oxen are hardworking, driven, and strong-willed—probably the first three words most people who know my mother would use to describe her. Not only is she an ox, she's also a Taurus, so no matter which zodiac you believe in, MeiYin Wong is one stubborn woman.

I, on the other hand, am a goat—creative, wandering, and disorganized. I'm also big on sleeping, watching TV, and just hanging out. I'm pretty much the polar opposite of my sister, Katie (a dragon, a born leader), and as you can imagine, none of my goatlike character traits go over very well with my mother. Still, I am her daughter, and sometimes, on very rare occasions, I summon the ox that lives deep down inside of me, too, and you'd be amazed how strong-willed and stubborn a lazy little goat can be.

Convincing my mother to take the cooking class with us is definitely a job for my inner ox. Luckily, he's super bored from not having been called on for so long and is ready to lock horns with a much bigger, more powerful beast. When Frankie and I got the text from Liza with the news about needing an adult, I was surprised at how determined I became to win the battle and sign up for the class. We *have* to be able to do this, and *I* have to help make it happen. I guess spending a month trying to fit in has made me kind of desperate—not exactly an oxlike quality, but powerful in its own way.

I'm helping my mother with the dishes when I mention the class. Our new house came with a perfectly good dishwasher, but my mother's not satisfied with the way it cleans, so she's ordered a new one. Until it arrives, she insists on doing the dishes by hand rather than using an appliance that isn't up to her standards. So we're both wearing rubber gloves, our arms elbow-deep in greasy suds, and I'm wondering what my mother has in store for me if I leave a few spots on the glasses like our dishwasher.

"How are those new friends of yours?" she asks while scouring the remains of some noodles that stuck to the bottom of a pot. "Are you going to invite them over again soon?"

"They were practically just here," I say. "And I told you, they aren't exactly friends. We're just doing a project together."

"How is the project going? There's a great library nearby. You can get there on your bicycle."

I put down the platter I've been rinsing and decide this is my moment. "Actually," I begin, turning to my mother, who has moved on to oiling a wok, "we're going to be doing a different kind of research for our project. We're taking a class."

My mother looks perplexed, but in a sort of angry way, as if confusion is a weakness that shouldn't be tolerated. "What do you mean taking a class? I thought the project was for one of the classes you're already taking."

"It is," I explain. "The project is for social studies. But we're going to do the research for it in a Saturday cooking class taught by a professional chef. It runs for six weeks, and we'll really learn a lot."

"A cooking class? *You?*" my mother says with the same tone of disbelief she'd use if I told her I was in the running for the Nobel Prize in science.

"I know I've never been that interested in

cooking, Mama, but this is a special kind of class. And it's for an assignment."

"Why do you need to take a special class? If you girls want to learn to cook, you could just ask me. I've been trying to show you how to make *jiǎozi* for years! Your friends certainly cleaned their plates, they must have liked my cooking."

"I know, Mama, they did. They loved the food you made. Everyone does. But this isn't a Chinese cooking class. We'll be learning all about *American* foods, traditional *American* foods, and how immigrants from all over the world brought them here."

"I see," my mother says, squirting out another blob of oil. "And you're doing this for a social studies class? Because *cooking* is an important part of American history?"

"Yes," I reply. "No. I mean, I don't know." I start spouting a bunch of things I think Mr. McEnroe would want to hear. "We have to come up with some aspect of immigration that would cut across all different groups. Some kind of 'common thread,' our teacher said. This is perfect! And all immigrants carried cooking traditions from back home with them to America. We're going to learn about what foods were brought here by which immigrant groups, about how common things we eat all the time are really from all over the world. We're going to base our project on that idea and make, you know, posters and a report and stuff to go with it." Actually, we haven't gotten as far as figuring out exactly what we're going to do yet, but she doesn't need to know that. "Maybe we'll make a cookbook or something," I add, a little lamely.

One thing you should know about my mother is that she doesn't use cookbooks. She learned to cook mostly by watching her own mother, my *lǎo lǎo*, and then just got better and better. It's like she has some kind of magical ability to know just what combination of ingredients will make something taste exactly the way she wants. There must be a hundred jars of dried herbs and smelly fermented fruits and vegetables in our cabinets, yet my mother can reach her hand in and find the one she needs without even looking. So it's not exactly surprising that she feels pretty much the same way about cookbooks as she does about ordering takeout.

Holding her glowing wok up for inspection, my mother offers one of her pronouncements. "The history of cooking in the United States—sounds very ambitious for a children's cooking class," she sniffs. "What kind of experience does the instructor have?"

I've just rinsed off the last bowl, and now I'm making little towers out of the soapsuds floating in the dirty water. "The teacher is a very famous chef," I explain. "He even has his own cooking show on TV."

My mother looks unimpressed, which doesn't surprise me. Other than the news and a Chinese soap opera she got addicted to last year when she broke her foot and was stuck in bed, she doesn't watch much TV. I'm the complete opposite, because I'll watch pretty much anything, even really boring sports like golf with my dad.

"And this *very famous chef* is teaching a cooking class just for children?" my mother asks, narrowing her eyes.

"Well," I say, demolishing my city of soapsuds, "not exactly." It's time to channel my inner ox. "It's not actually a children's class. It's an *adult* class that will allow kids. Kids accompanied by an adult. And I was thinking maybe we could take it together."

At first the next part of the conversation goes exactly as I expected it would. My mother looks at me like I'm crazy, sighs, and says she doesn't need someone else to teach her how to cook. I tell her that I know she's good, but taking the class is really important to me, that we can't take it without her, and can't she just do this one thing that I want?

My mother hangs the wok on its hook and walks back over to the sink, where I'm still watching the tiny soap bubbles pop one by one in the oily dishwater. I peek up to test the atmosphere. She's staring at me, and I can see her face soften. "Yang Yang," she says, using my Chinese name, "I have no need to learn to cook these foods. We are Chinese."

Suddenly, I feel a sharp pain in my stomach. It lasts only a second or two, but I know right away what it is: a kick from the tiny ox inside me, reminding me to stand my ground.

"Well," I begin, "you may be Chinese, but I'm both. Chinese and American. You chose to stay here, and you chose to have us here, so you chose for me to be both. And right now I want us to learn about American traditions too." She doesn't seem to be weakening, so I throw out my last, desperate argument. "Or are you afraid you won't be as good at American cooking as you are at Chinese?"

Nothing in my mom's expression changes except her jaw, which tightens as she makes a tiny clicking sound in her throat. She makes this sound very effectively—and often—to show irritation or to herd us where she wants us to go. But right now it tells me she's trying to decide whether or not to get really angry. Her inner Taurus the Bull has taken over for the ox, and I'm the one holding the red scarf.

"Don't be ridiculous, Lillian. If I can make bird's nest soup, I'm quite sure I can make a French fry or a hamburger patty."

I may not be able to tighten my jaw and click as well as she can, but when I put my hand on one hip, I can look pretty fierce. "Okay then, Mama," I say, "prove it."

Even a slacker goat like me knows that a bull rarely says no to a challenge. My mother flares her nostrils like the massive hoofed creatures within her. This is it: The class, the project, and my best shot at making friends so far this year all depend on whether my mother decides to charge or hold her ground.

Mama locks eyes with me for another long moment. Then, slowly, the corners of her mouth begin to rise. She's smiling, but there's a glint in her eye that's not entirely friendly. Goat and I have won.

"Fine," she says, holding out her hand for me to shake. "As you girls would say, it's a deal."

I'm so happy that I start jumping up and down. Instead of shaking her hand, I throw my arms around my mother's neck, leap up, and wrap my legs around her waist. Just like in a TV show, my father and Katie choose that very moment to enter the kitchen. The sight of my five-foot-three mother holding her five-foot-one daughter must be so ridiculous that it stops them in their tracks. They stare at us for a minute, then turn to each other and exchange a bewildered look. Finally, my father—who does math all day and is a man of few words—clears his throat. "Well," he says to Katie, handing her a clean teacup from the dish rack before taking one for himself, "looks like they've finished with the dishes."

# CHAPTER 13

## *Liza*

Believe it or not, whoever came up with the quote on that poster in the school infirmary wasn't completely clueless. Wednesday night I got almost simultaneous texts after dinner from both Frankie and Lillian: Their moms said yes—both of them. Of course I was relieved that we could take the class, but suddenly, I was the only one whose mom was still holding out—and *my* mom taking the class with us was the entire part two of my original big idea.

The next day, after we'd all registered and paid for the class, I'd pretty much given up hope that my mom would sign up, and I was getting ready to be the latchkey kid of American Cooking 101. But all that imagining and dreaming I did must have paid off, because that night my mom came home looking seriously annoyed. After she put Cole to bed, she told me about how she'd spent the whole afternoon arguing with clients who just wouldn't listen to her and had gotten on her last nerve. Later, when we were eating dinner, the commercial for the class came on again, and just like that, Mom shook her head, put down her fork, and said, "You know what, Lize? I'm going to take that class." She even booked Cammy, the ninth grader who lives upstairs from us, to babysit for Cole on Saturday afternoons.

That was Thursday. Now it's Saturday and we're supposed to be leaving for class, only Cammy's mom just called to say that Cammy has a fever and won't be able to babysit. She offered to watch Cole herself, but he can be seriously cranky with people he doesn't know, so Mom told her that she should stay home in case Cammy needs her and that we'd figure out something to do with Cole. That "something" turned out to be taking him along with us. I hope the chef likes babies—and that there are safety knobs on the stoves.

"Okay, everybody, let's do this," my mom says, zipping up the diaper bag. From all the toys, snacks, and extra clothes she's stuffed it with, you'd think we were going away for the weekend instead of a few hours. But that's life with a two-and-a-half-year-old. Mom grabs the stroller and I scoop up Cole, who's waving around his sippy cup and splashing milk all over the apartment.

"I'll take that, mister," I say, snatching the cup out of Cole's hands and switching it with a box of animal crackers. The guy is a sugar fiend, and I've discovered that the trick to getting him to cooperate is just to keep giving him sweets. My mom's not crazy about that plan, but this was supposed to be *my* afternoon with her, so there's no way I'm feeling guilty about a few little crackers.

We decide to walk to the cooking studio because it's warm and sunny out today, but Cole whines and fusses the whole way there and my mom and I are feeling anything but "sunny" when we arrive. Frankie and Lillian and their moms are already standing around a big metal table in the middle of the room, which is huge, with fancy-looking steel appliances lining three of the walls. The other wall is all windows and looks right out onto the street. Even though we won't be on TV, I guess we'll kind of be starring in a cooking show of our own, at least for the people passing by on the sidewalk.

Chef Antonio comes to meet us at the door, and all I can say is, *Wow!* He's even better-looking in person, and I can already tell that he's just as friendly in real life. Cole starts howling and struggling to escape his stroller the minute we're inside, but Chef

Antonio's smile doesn't fade as he holds out his hand to me first and then my mom.

"Welcome to my kitchen," he says in a deep, Spanish-accented voice that sounds so familiar, like he's an old friend instead of a stranger I've only seen on TV. "I'm Antonio, and you must be Liza and Ms. Reynolds." He waves his hand toward the big table. "Your friends have been telling me all about you."

"Call me Jackie," my mom says while trying to get Cole to calm down.

I give Frankie a look that says, *You'd better not have said anything embarrassing.* Frankie's mom—who insists that I call her Theresa, even though it still feels a little strange—looks at us, then at Frankie, and then back at us. She waves at my mom and then whispers something to Frankie with a confused expression on her face. I guess Frankie "forgot" to mention that my mom decided at the last minute to take the class after all. I catch Lillian's eye as her mom is hissing something in her ear too. Looks like my big idea has morphed into some kind of mother-daughter cooking adventure—probably not what our moms were expecting, but too many is better than not enough!

Next to Dr. Wong is someone I don't recognize, and I notice for the first time that along with Frankie, Lillian, and their moms, there are four other people at the table: two men around my dad's age and a couple who are definitely married (or at least boyfriend and girlfriend) because they're holding hands and looking at each other in that same goofy, dreamy way Frankie stares at Mr. McEnroe. They're all staring at us, of course, wondering what kind of people would bring a wailing baby to a grown-up cooking class.

Chef Antonio squats down in front of Cole's stroller, which is literally rocking and rolling thanks to my brother's nonstop squirming. This is not exactly the first impression I was hoping to make. "And what's your name, little man?" the chef asks him, smiling and holding out his hand as if Cole were a grown-up instead of a bratty toddler. Cole pushes his hand away and tries even harder to wriggle out of his stroller harness, and Chef Antonio stands back up. He's still smiling, but I bet he wishes Cole would shut up already.

My mom sighs and shoots me an "I told you so" look. She smiles apologetically at the others and turns to Chef Antonio. "I'm sorry," she says, pushing Cole back into his seat and tightening the straps. "Our babysitter got sick. I'll just walk him around the block a few times, and maybe he'll take a nap. Please get started without me, and Liza will catch me up on what I've missed."

"Mom—," I start to say, but before I have a chance to argue, she's wheeled the stroller around and is pushing it out the door, Cole still whining his little head off.

Chef Antonio puts his arm around my shoulder like we're old friends and leads me toward the table where the rest of the class is waiting. "Not to worry, Liza," he says, and I can hear the smile in his voice again. "Your mom will be back before you know it. Come, join your friends and meet some new ones!"

Frankie runs up to us and grabs my hand, pulling me over to the table. "Finally!" she says. "I thought you were going to ditch us!"

"Well," I say, "it looks like my mom just might have." Frankie's mom gives me a little hug and looks after the closing door like she wishes she could make a run for it too.

"No way," Frankie says, bumping Lillian out of the way so I can squeeze in next to her at the table. "I'm sure Cole will chill out soon and she'll be back in a few."

I step back so Lillian isn't smushed between me and her mom, who's looking around the room with her lips pursed like she's a health inspector or the judge in an interior design competition. She's also eyeing Theresa and the spot where my mom vanished, like she's been tricked. "Nice to see you, Dr. Wong," I say, attempting to smooth things out. "And sorry, Lillian, I didn't mean to crash into you. Sometimes Frankie gets a little hyper."

"I do not!" says Frankie. But she knows she totally does. "Aren't you going to sit next to me, Lize?" she asks, which is pretty rude considering that Lillian is already there.

I give Lillian a "Don't worry about her" look. "I think I should sit over there next to the empty seat and wait for my mom," I tell Frankie. "You know, since I begged her to take the class and everything." I start to walk off when it hits me, and I turn back to Frankie and Lillian. "Shouldn't one of us be taking notes or something for our project?"

Lillian smiles with a look in her eyes that reminds me of our old cat when he'd hidden a "present" for us under the doormat (trust me, you don't want to know!). "I've got it covered," she says, and pulls one of those tiny digital video recorders out of her pocket. "As soon as the chef starts talking, I start taping."

"Sweet!" I tell her, looking over at Frankie. Even she can't help being impressed.

I make my way over to the other side of the table, where Frankie's mom and the two men are chatting it up. I pull up a chair between the empty seat and one of the men, who has skin even darker than my mom's and a very carefully trimmed grayish beard. "Salt-and-pepper" is the way I've heard people describe hair like his. He smiles at me, and I like the way the corners of his eyes crinkle behind the dark green frames of his glasses.

"Hi," I say, holding out my hand like Chef Antonio did when he met us at the door. "I'm Liza."

"Well, hello," the man says, shaking my hand. "I'm Henry, and this is Errol." He gestures toward the friendly-looking, red-haired man next to him, who's now talking to the lovebirds at the end of the table. "I'm supposed to be here with my mom," I explain. "and *not* my little brother."

Henry shakes his head and laughs. "I have five

little brothers, my dear. Been there, done that."

I smile for probably the first time since Cammy's mom called this morning.

"I see you're here with your friends, though," Henry says. "Friends are usually better than brothers." He elbows Errol in the arm. "I've been friends with this guy since we were about your age." I'm definitely liking Henry already.

I don't really meet Errol because he's still talking to the guy and the girl (or woman, I guess), who I now notice are wearing shiny rings that look brand new. I decide to call them "the Newlyweds." They laugh a lot and look really psyched just to be together. I try to picture my mom and dad looking that happy to be with each other, but I can't. I have to go way back to remember a time when they weren't fighting about something.

While we're all introducing ourselves, Chef Antonio sets something up at a counter along the wall, then comes back and stands at the head of the table, rubbing his hands together. My mom must have sensed that class was about to start, because here she comes now, shoving the door to the cooking studio open with her back and dragging the stroller in behind her. And guess what? Cole is still fussing and crying! Before he was born, I begged for a little brother or sister, but right now I seriously miss being an only child.

Everyone stops talking and turns to look at Cole and my mom, who has clearly had it. "I'm very sorry," she says, looking first at Chef Antonio and then at me, "but this just isn't going to work. Maybe next time."

*Huh?* I slide off my chair and run to the door. "Wait, Mom, you're going to miss the first class? But you signed up and everything. . . . " I sound as whiny as Cole.

"I said I was sorry, honey, but look at your brother. And besides," she says, gesturing to the staring crowd at the table, "your friends' moms are here, you don't really need me."

I give Cole a look that scares him so much he actually stops crying . . . for about five seconds. "But, Mom," I whisper, trying not to sound like a toddler, "I do need you."

"I've got to get him out of here, Lize," my mom says, like she didn't even hear me. "We'll be back to pick you up at three." She wheels the stroller around and heads for the door, nearly crashing into two people who have chosen this exact moment to enter the studio.

*"Dónde está el fuego?"* says a short woman with curly black hair and long, colorful earrings. I've taken only a month of Spanish so far, but even I know that means "Where's the fire?" The woman places her hands on the stroller handles to avoid a collision, then looks up at my mom, who is clearly frazzled.

"Oh my," my mom says. "Excuse me, I'm so sorry." Cole lets out a scream, and I wonder if Mom's going to start crying too.

The woman looks down at Cole, and a warm smile spreads across her face. Without saying anything to my mom, she bends over the stroller and starts unbuckling the harness. She doesn't seem to notice how obnoxious Cole is acting—or how completely embarrassed my mom and I feel. Beneath her heavy, perfectly done makeup, her face is wrinkled but beautiful. Up close you can see the gray roots around the part in her hair. It's impossible to know whether this woman is fifty or seventy, but you can tell she was supermodel gorgeous when she was younger.

"*Ay, chiquito,*" the woman says, sliding Cole's arms out of the straps and lifting him out of the stroller in a gentle but sure way that tells me she's done this loads of times before. "*Qué pasa, papi?*"she asks Cole, bouncing him a little bit and tickling his neck.

Whoever she is, this lady is clearly a baby whisperer, because my brother immediately cuts out the Terrible Two-ness and magically transforms into the happy, giggly Cole who attracts people in grocery stores like he is a free sample. "Yummy," they always say when they see his chubby cheeks. The two of them dance off toward a corner of the kitchen where there's a smaller table and a couple of chairs. Whoa, I'm impressed.

Left standing at the door facing Cole's empty stroller and my mom is a boy who looks around my age. He's carrying a backpack and wearing earphones that connect to a phone in his hand.

Chef Antonio appears and takes the stroller from my mom with one hand and yanks the headphones from the boy's ears with the other. Motioning to me, he leads us over to the corner where the baby whisperer is still tangoing with my brother. "Jackie, Liza, meet *mi mamacita*, my mother," he says, putting his arm around the shoulders of the woman holding Cole.

"Call me Angelica," she says in a thick accent, pronouncing the *g* like an *h*. I'd believe it if she told us she really is an angel, the way she's charmed Cole, who doesn't even seem to notice my mom or me.

The boy plunks his backpack down on one of the little tables and slumps down into a chair. He starts pushing buttons on his phone until Chef Antonio reaches down and grabs it. He puts the phone in his chef's apron pocket and rests his hand on the boy's head. "And this bundle of energy is my son, Javier," he says. "Javier, say hello to our new students."

Javier forces a smile and gives us a quick wave. Chef Antonio tugs at one of his curls, and Javier pushes his hand away. "Quit it, Papi!" he says.

Chef Antonio pats the pocket that holds Javier's phone. "Start doing your homework and you can have this back after class."

Javier sighs and reaches for his backpack as my mom reaches out to take Cole from Angelica. "Thank you so much," she says. "I'll take him now."

"Don't be silly," Chef Antonio's mother says, waving us off toward the big table, where the rest of the class is sitting, staring at us. I notice that she wears big silver rings on almost all of her fingers and her long nails are painted a deep red that matches her lipstick exactly. "Go on, enjoy yourselves, *chicas. Mi amigo* and

I will be just fine." She dips Cole like they're a team on *Dancing with the Stars,* and he lets out a sparkly laugh.

My mother and I look at each other and shrug. I'd rather Cole was at home with Cammy so I could have Mom all to myself, but if Angelica can keep him under her spell for the rest of the class, I'll take it. My mom takes one last look at Cole and then turns back to me and smiles. We take our seats next to Henry and Errol.

Chef Antonio stands at the head of the table in front of a cutting board and the fancy case where he keeps his knives (I think it's the same one he uses on TV!). "Ladies and gentlemen," he begins, "*Señoras y señores.* Welcome to Antonio's Kitchen, where fresh is best and a little spice is oh-so-nice."

That's exactly what he says at the beginning of every show, and we all burst into applause after he says it, as if we were in the studio audience.

Chef Antonio laughs. *"Por favor, mis amigos,"* he says, looking around the table at each of us, "no need for applause. We're going to be together for six weeks. If you give me an ovation after everything I say, we won't have time for cooking—or, more importantly, eating!"

Everyone laughs, except for Dr. Wong, who's giving Chef Antonio the same narrow-eyed look she gave the rest of the room. I glance at Lillian to see if she notices, but she's got her camera out and is too busy recording the chef's every word to pay attention to her mother. She looks happy just to be here and to have convinced her mom to come along. Suddenly, I realize that I feel exactly the same way, and I exhale the breath it feels like I've been holding since we walked into the studio with Cole screaming bloody murder. Maybe my big idea wasn't so dumb after all. Who knows? So far the *If you can dream it, you can achieve it* poster hasn't steered me wrong.

# CHAPTER 14
## *Frankie*

"We're going to begin our adventures in American cooking with this," Chef Antonio announces, brandishing an unpeeled ear of corn. "Corn, or maize, is actually indigenous to the Americas and was introduced to the European explorers by the native populations."

Now that I'm actually here in the room with him, I totally get what Liza sees in Chef Antonio. His skin is the color of the caramel swirl in dulce de leche ice cream, and he has a way of looking at you with those big dark eyes that makes your insides start to melt. He's no Mr. Mac, but with that accent, he makes even words like "indigenous" and "native populations" sound sexy.

"The Europeans brought corn back to their own countries," Chef continues, "and it spread from there. It did not take long for this hardy crop to become a staple of cuisines around the world."

Across from me, I see Dr. Wong turn the video camera Lillian's holding so it's facing her. "Corn has been part of the Chinese diet since the fourteenth century," she whispers loudly into the camera.

"Mama!" Lillian shout-whispers back. She rolls her eyes and points the camera at Chef Antonio again.

"That," Dr. Wong sniffs, "could be important information for your project."

I hold back a snort. All three of us taking this class with our moms might turn out to be more entertaining than I expected. Actually, I'm sure there are a few other adjectives I could come up with to describe my mom's behavior since we arrived.

The very first thing she did when we walked through the door was tell Chef Antonio that her cooking skills are "underappreciated" by her family. As if she has any skills for us to appreciate—under or not! Then I heard her sharing some jewels from the family collection of "Mom in the Kitchen" tales. She does that when she meets people; she becomes super confessional to win them over, to get them on her side. I know the theory—poke fun at yourself first, then other people won't need to—but it drives me nuts. Chef winked at me, so I'm thinking he's probably been through this before. Hopefully he can work some magic on my mom's cooking the way his mother cast her spell on Liza's little brother, Cole.

"Before we get started on our first recipe," Chef tells us, "I want each of you to get up close and personal with today's main ingredient. We have a nice, even group of ten in our class, which means we're going to be working in pairs. In front of each pair you'll see one of these." He holds up a small marble bowl and cylinder. "Does anyone know what we call this tool?"

"A mortar and pestle," Lillian's mom answers in a flash. "Used for grinding herbs and spices." She looks proud of herself, as if we're having a contest to see who can answer first. And Liza thinks *I'm* competitive!

"In our house those things are considered weapons," my mom says. "We have a set, but my husband has to hide it so my boys don't grind anyone's fingers into paste." Oh, man. Now she's starting in on the "Crazy Caputos" stories?

Everyone chuckles, except Dr. Wong, who clearly wanted to get credit for her correct answer. It's weird, but I've been in situations where I've felt exactly the same way.

"Well, class," Chef Antonio says, "today we're going to use this dangerous weapon—one of the oldest cooking tools historians have recorded—to create cornmeal, which is the base for many different dishes in cultures from around the world. Actually, it was first used to feed cattle, but then folks realized, 'Hey, this stuff is *too good*.'"

Chef shows us the prep table, where all sorts of ingredients are laid out in dishes and bowls, and tells us to fill a tiny glass bowl with dried corn kernels and bring it back to our partners. Liza and I dip our tiny bowls into the kernels at the same time, scooping up any old amount, but Dr. Wong makes Lillian do it in this very careful, precise way, even though we're not actually measuring anything. Lillian looks so embarrassed that I almost feel sorry for her—until I remember that she's totally intruding on my friendship with Liza.

As the chef demonstrates, I try to watch the way he grinds the kernels in a neat, even—what Mr. McEnroe would call "fluid"—way. He says, "No need for rat-a-tat-tat movements. See? Nice and easy. . . ."

Back at the table with my mom, I pour our dried

corn into the marble bowl. "Do you want to go first?" I ask.

"Why not?" my mom says. "I can't burn them, right?"

"Right," I say, trying to sound positive, even though overcooking is just one of the many ways my mom regularly inflicts damage in the kitchen.

I look around, and everyone is getting into the rhythm of grinding their corn, cool as cucumbers. And then there's my mom, pounding away at our kernels, bits and pieces flying everywhere except in the bowl. I wish I'd worn safety goggles.

Mom finishes "grinding" and looks up from our pathetic mess. She glances around at everyone else pretending not to notice. "Oops," she says, a little too cheerfully.

Chef Antonio comes around to our side of the table and puts one hand on my mom's shoulder and the other on mine. I make eye contact with Liza, who makes goo-goo eyes and mouths the word "lucky."

"Ay, ay, ay, ladies," Chef says, eyeing my mom's latest disaster, "what happened over here?"

My mom sweeps as much of the corn shrapnel as she can into her hand and dumps it into the mortar. "I'm not sure," she says, "but I'll definitely get the hang of it next time."

Chef laughs warmly and gives my mom a supportive pat on the shoulder. "Fortunately for you, Theresa, that was just a little project to give you all a sense of the process for turning corn into cornmeal, which can then be transformed into almost anything. Our first recipe starts with a combination of cornmeal and water, which in many places is eaten just like that and referred to as 'cereal' or 'porridge' or— my favorite—'mush.'"

In a kind of bizarre unison, Liza, Lillian, and I make faces at the idea of eating wet, soggy cornmeal—the image of cows chewing mush cud is now burned into my brain—and everyone laughs.

"Don't worry, girls." Chef Antonio beams at us.

"You will be surprised at just how delicious a lowly mush can be when in the right hands. All over the world people transform it into something marvelous. The Romanians have *sadza*, the Brazilians *angu*— everybody loves it in some form or other!"

"Now, Theresa, since you mentioned earlier that you grew up with Italian cooking, our first recipe should be a piece of cake—or, I should say, a piece of *polenta*—for you."

Great. Since my mom's track record isn't terribly impressive when it comes to simple tasks like boiling water for pasta, I'm pretty sure that the fact that a dish is Italian won't give her any sort of culinary advantage. But I go along with her idea that she's the "head chef" and I'm the "sous chef," handing her ingredients the way E.R. nurses hand surgeons scalpels and clamps on hospital shows.

To her credit, my mom doesn't burn the polenta. Unfortunately, that's only because it takes her so long to get the lumps out. You have to whisk the cornmeal into the boiling water delicately, slowly, evenly to avoid creating balls of the stuff. My mom pretty much dumps it in. So we have both little hard pellets that might break your teeth and larger marble-size ones that explode with a cough-inducing puff of powder. Not so tasty to eat that, I'm sure. But she doesn't burn it, since the rest of the class has moved on to the next recipe before we have a chance to put ours in the oven.

The next item is Mexican corn on the cob with butter, lime, and Cotija cheese—the kind we line up to buy at the food carts surrounding the old soccer field across from the city pool. This she burns. Actually, it's more like she incinerates it.

Our final recipe of the day is corn bread—one of my dad's firehouse specials. Dad's corn bread is even more famous in our family than his waffles. It also happens to be one of the recipes that I've been making with him since I was little. I've never tried, but I could probably make Dad's corn bread from memory. My mom knows this, of course. Even though the two of us don't have the kind of partner ESP like Liza and I do, without saying a word, we switch positions so that now she's the sous chef and I'm in charge.

Despite the fact that my mom nearly mixed up the measurements for sugar and salt, then splashed the buttermilk everywhere, our corn bread comes out pretty good. It's not Dad-quality, but it's definitely edible, which is more than I can say for the dishes Mom attempted. Chef Antonio is working his way around the room, tasting everyone's bread and giving out compliments and pointers. When he reaches us, his eyes light up at the sight of our perfectly golden, fully cooked corn bread.

"You see, Theresa," he says, putting his arm around my mom's shoulders (if Liza weren't focusing on her corn bread, she'd be really jealous!), "the third time is a charm. Just look at this gorgeous creation. I knew you could do it—you should be proud!"

Poor Mom. Chef Antonio has moved along to Errol and Henry before we have the chance to set him straight. It doesn't matter anyway. I'm sure my mom's cooking "challenges" will reveal themselves again next week—over and over again.

# CHAPTER 15
## *Lillian*

Going to school with your mother is definitely weird, even if it is *cooking* school. Mama has never been shy about her (very) extensive knowledge of food, but who knew she'd be like one of those kids who always raises a hand aggressively or blurts out the answer without giving anyone else a chance? It's like she just wants to show off how much she knows about every little thing. So embarrassing.

At least she didn't turn every recipe into a disaster,

like Frankie's mom. But I think I might have preferred that to how competitive she was—with me—and how she insisted on doing everything perfectly. By the look on Frankie's face at the end of class, I'm guessing she would have rather been partners with my mother than hers. I'm beginning to discover that those two have a lot in common. Maybe that's why Frankie's still not even half as nice to me as Liza. I can tell she's trying, but mostly because Liza's always giving her looks or nudges to remind her that we're all a team.

Right now we're in the computer lab at school. We're supposed to be writing up our project proposal for Mr. McEnroe, but we got preoccupied looking at the video I shot of Saturday's class. I mostly focused on Chef Antonio explaining the history of corn and demonstrating how to do the tricky parts of the recipes, but I also got some good action shots of Liza, Frankie, and their moms.

"Hey, there's my polenta!" Liza yells, pointing at

the screen but being careful not to touch it because our digital media teacher, Mr. Russo, makes you clean every single monitor in the room if he catches you even *accidentally* touching one. "Looking good, right? And tasty, too!"

"I'll bet," Frankie grumbles. She's already fast-forwarded through the shots of her mom stirring and stirring—technically, we were "whisking"—their lumpy pot of polenta. Her mom looks more like she is literally attacking the cornmeal than preparing it. On the screen we can see her go whack, whack, whack. Apparently, they never made it past the "mush" stage.

I didn't shoot much of Mama and me working on our recipes, mostly because it was hard to hold the camera and add ingredients at the same time. The few shots I did get make me cringe. In every one my mother is showing me how to "properly" sprinkle herbs or pour batter into a baking dish—or even spread butter on corn! I'm starting to wonder if asking her to sign up for the class was a mistake. She was ready to quit as soon as she found out the other moms were taking it too, but I'd dared her to take the class and she'd accepted. And MeiYin Wong never walks away from a challenge.

"Those two are all over each other," Liza says as we watch the couple she calls "the Newlyweds" taste their corn bread. They actually feed each other little bites like it's wedding cake and they're the bride and groom all over again. "I hope I'm that happy when I get married."

They do look happy. My parents never show that kind of affection for each other. Their lives are completely intertwined and I can't imagine one of them existing without the other (what would my father eat? who would my mother talk to about the superiority of Chinese everything?), but I can't remember ever seeing them kiss on the lips (*ew!*) or even hold hands.

Frankie points to something in the corner of the screen behind the Newlyweds, and Liza and I lean in to get a closer look. "There's Chef's son," she says. "Javier, right? Total cuteness."

In the frame Javier is not just tiny but also blurry, and Liza leans in even closer. "Really? Headphone Boy? I barely even noticed him, what with Cole throwing a hissy fit and then Angelica doing her fairy godmother thing."

I don't say anything, but I definitely noticed Javier. He has the same thick curls and deep brown eyes as his dad, and—the one time I caught him doing it—a really sweet smile. Sometimes when Chef Antonio was giving us instructions or my mother was going on about why her methods are "better" than his, I kept the camera focused on the action and let my eyes wander over to the little table in the corner of the studio where Javier was hunched over his notebook.

"What about you, Lillian?" Frankie asks. "What did you think of Javier?"

"Um . . ." I shrug, trying to look natural. "He seemed okay."

Frankie narrows her eyes and then turns to Liza. "She's blushing! I think Lillian has a crush on Javier!"

Liza shoots her a look. "Frankie."

"No, I don't!" I insist, probably too strongly. "I didn't even talk to him."

"Hmm." Frankie looks unconvinced. "We'll have to fix that next week."

"No, really," I plead. "Please don't." But it's kind of nice to have Frankie teasing me about something . . . maybe she's starting to warm up to me?

"Hey, Frankie," Liza says, directing our attention back to the screen, "check out your corn bread!" In my head I thank her for changing the subject.

The next shot is of Chef Antonio congratulating Frankie and her mom on their drama-free final recipe. Mrs. Caputo has a fine dusting of cornmeal throughout her hair, and her apron is covered with streaks of char. She's smiling at the chef, but her heart clearly isn't in it.

"You made that, didn't you, Franks?" asks Liza.

"Your dad and the rest of Engine Company Nine would be proud."

"Should I put corn bread on our list of foods we'll include in our project for the museum?" I ask, doing my best to make sure the conversation stays on food and project planning and doesn't veer back to boys.

Frankie's eyes start to roll, but she controls herself with great effort. "Sorry, Lillian, but how is corn bread an example of a food that was brought *to* America *by* immigrants? It was the Native Americans who taught the European settlers how to make it, remember?"

"Oh yeah, right," I say, ignoring the attitude and trying to stay positive. She may not like me very much, but I'm determined to figure Frankie out. Winning her over and becoming real friends with her and Liza would be even better than getting an A+ on our project. I decide to make it my personal challenge, and, like my mom, I refuse to back down.

# CHAPTER 16
## *Liza*

My mom is a hotshot editor for a parenting magazine, so I'm used to her coming home from work stressed out at the end of the day. But when Mom walks in the door, shoves Cole in my arms, goes straight to her room, and slams the door without even taking off her jacket, it means she's having a *really* bad day. And today is one of those.

Luckily, Cole is completely oblivious to my mom's moods. As soon as I'm holding him, he starts pulling my hair over my eyes and trying to play peekaboo while I stumble around blindly, hoping not to topple over and send us both crashing into the glass coffee table. My mom, the parenting magazine editor, has been meaning to "babyproof" our home since Cole started crawling a year and a half ago. It's one of many things she "means" to do but hasn't gotten around to yet.

"Hey, quit it!" I yell, which sends my brother into convulsions of wild cackling, making it even harder to keep us upright.

Unzipping Cole's sweatshirt is like peeling a banana that keeps slipping out of your hand, but I eventually manage to pin him to the couch and wrestle it off. Frankie and I made a deal that we'd get into exercising this year, but we haven't officially gotten started. I wonder if chasing a two-year-old all over our apartment for twenty minutes counts as a workout. I think about Frankie at home with her brothers and realize that she probably won't be impressed.

The one thing that calms my brother down every time is watching Elmo on my mom's phone. I show him the phone so he knows what's coming and am able to settle him into his high chair without breaking another sweat. While Cole sings along with Elmo, I poke around our nearly empty freezer for something to make him for dinner. We're out of hot dogs, so I heat up some frost-covered chicken nuggets in the microwave (they're organic, but they actually taste as good as the fast-food kind). I hope those reports you sometimes hear about microwaved food not being safe to eat aren't true, because I can't remember the last time Cole ate anything hot that was cooked any other way. There are no clean sippy cups in sight, so I pour some milk into a coffee mug and tell Cole he's going to drink like a big boy tonight. He looks at me, nodding, all excited cuteness.

By the time my mom comes out of her room, there's ketchup on her phone and a smashed mug on the floor. I should have looked harder for a sippy cup.

She stands in the doorway watching me sweep up the broken pieces and shaking her head. The part of the mug that says #1 MOM is still intact, so I hand it to her, which makes her laugh. "You keep it," she says, pressing it into my hand. "You earned it tonight."

Cole wails when Mom grabs her sticky phone out of his even stickier hands and hollers even louder as she wipes ketchup and grease off his face with one of our scratchier kitchen towels. "You said it, mister," she tells him in a voice that says she feels like screaming bloody murder too, and then she scoops him out of the chair and heads to the bathroom.

I check the fridge in case there are any leftovers still around, even though I know we finished off the last crumbs yesterday. Believe it or not, it's been four days since we've ordered in for dinner. After cooking class on Saturday, we went to the food co-op and filled up our cart with "real" groceries—as in, things that don't come in a box in the freezer section—which my mom actually cooked. On Saturday night she sautéed chicken with mushrooms—one of her old favorites—and poured it over our polenta. Mmmmm. And on Sunday she made a huge pot of chili—spicy but not too spicy—that we've been eating with the corn bread every night since.

It looks like it's back to the menu drawer for us tonight, though. I dig around for the one from the ramen place on Smith Street while my mom finishes up Cole's bath. When she's in a mood, Mom craves comfort food, and there's nothing more comforting than a big bowl of noodles in steaming, salty broth. Until a few months ago I didn't know there was more to ramen than the kind that comes in a plastic wrapper and costs a quarter at the corner deli. But the place we order from is a whole restaurant devoted to ramen, where the noodles are handmade and the soup is topped with crunchy vegetables and smoky bits of pork or chicken. My mom gets hers with an egg cracked on top, which sizzles and turns milky white when it touches the broth. I prefer mine without the egg but with an extra square of toasted seaweed on the side. Ramen like that costs a lot more than a quarter, but it's worth it—especially if it makes my mom smile after the kind of day she must have had today.

I order our food and hear the froggy night-light switch on in Cole's room right after I hang up the phone. My mom comes into the living room wearing her sweatpants and carrying a big stack of magazines in her arms. She plops the pile onto the coffee table. Each issue has a rainbow of sticky tabs poking out from the top, bottom, and sides. It's sort of funny—"ironic," my dad would say— that my mom works at a parenting magazine that's all about "family time," creativity, and doing stuff together, but she's never had time to do things like make holiday crafts with us or hand-paint borders in our rooms or even put together a proper baby album. That's pretty much what the whole mag- azine is about. She tries hard to not bring work home with her at night, but I know from experi-ence that all those stickies mean there's a big issue coming up, and we'll probably be seeing even less of her than usual.

"Holiday double issue closes a week from Friday," she says, flipping through the magazine on top of the pile. "And the bigwigs at the publishing company just asked us to change our entire editorial plan."

"Ugh," I say, looking through the stack of old holiday issues for the one that includes a picture of me as a baby, popping out of a green polka-dot box with big red bows tied in my pigtails. Apparently, it took a full hour to get me to smile for the camera, which is why that was my first, last, and only photo shoot.

"Ugh is right. Looks like I'll be working all week-end, which means I'm going to have to miss our cook-ing class on Saturday. Good thing I have Cammy booked to watch Cole. And she better not be sick this time around."

"What?" I plop the magazines back down on the stack. "But you can't miss the cooking class, Mom. There are only six and you promised!"

My mom puts down her magazine and takes my hand, giving it a little squeeze. "I know I did, Liza, and I'm sorry. Believe me, I'd much rather be cooking with you than thinking up 'Fifteen Things to Do with Leftover Christmas Cookies' and 'How to Make Your Own Hanukkah/Kwanzaa Candle Crayons,' but I have no choice. A deadline's a deadline."

"It's only two hours," I plead, unable to control the whine in my voice. "You'll need to take a break sometime, won't you?"

"Two hours is a long break, Lize. Plus the time it takes to walk to and from the cooking studio. I'll do my very best to be there for the next one, sweetheart, but this week you're just going to have to triple up with Frankie and Theresa or Lillian and her mom. It'll be fun. It's just slicing and dicing, anyway. You don't really need me.

"Think of it this way"—she takes my chin in her hand—"I'm sure Theresa would appreciate all the help she can get."

I make a weak attempt at smiling and am relieved when the doorbell rings and my mom gets up to pay for our food. While she's in the kitchen pouring our soup into bowls, I take a thick black Sharpie marker out of her pen cup and draw mustaches on the "cover moms" on every magazine in the pile. Immature? Maybe. It's not like I'm messing up anything important; the magazines are all old issues that have already been published. But my mom keeps her work things neat and orderly, so she'll definitely be annoyed.

Just like me.

# CHAPTER 17
## *Frankie*

This is so not going the way I wanted. Mr. Mac has let us have the end of class to work on our projects. If our proposals are accepted, we can move on to actual work. If not, he'll circulate and help. Much as I would have loved his one-on-one help, our proposal was *awesome*. His word, not mine. Written in big red letters across the top of our paper: *Awesome!*

Sigh.

Now we have to transform the awesome idea into

awesome reality, and I am not liking the prospects for that. Liza and me, we're a dream team. We work well together, we work hard, and we usually agree on what to do. And we always have *awesome* results.

Today, though, Liza is down and not helping at all, because her mom is bailing on this week's class. No surprise there. I'm actually surprised her mom made it to a single class, but I don't say that. I know she's bummed—I get it—but the real point of the cooking class is to help us devastate this assignment, not bond with our mothers. And, anyway, right now we have to make a "blueprint," as Mr. Mac says. A blueprint for our project.

"Guys," I say, interrupting Liza and Lillian's ongoing heart-to-heart about Liza's mom. "We've got to get this project mapped out. Sophie, Carmen, and Oliver are already meeting at lunch every day." This might not be totally true, but I want these two to focus. "Okay, I was thinking we want tons going on in our booth, right? Lots of variety, stuff for people to look at and read so that ours is the best. So what do we think: at least two dioramas of immigrants with the food they introduced to the U.S.? Liza and I will make those. A couple papier-mâché pieces of food? All over it—I've already started hoarding newspaper. We'll need to write up the descriptions and maybe grab people's attention with some old photos or illustrations. We can handle that, right, Lize?"

Liza puffs out her cheeks to blow the little fly-away hairs that escape from her braids out of her eyes. "Frankie, look around the table. What exactly do you suggest that Lillian do?" She laughs sort of nervously and glances over at Lillian. "I think you forgot that there are three people in our group this time, didn't you?"

*As if.* Lillian appears at lunchtime. She shadows Liza in the hallway. She is totally around *all* the time. Forget her? Not likely.

Liza goes on. "Have you seen the drawings Lillian does on the inside of her notebooks? Like the one she's doing of the back of Mr. Mac's head right now? She just churns them out all the time. This girl is an artist. Lillian should do the illustrations for sure, since neither one of us can really draw. And we can make the papier-mâché pieces together at my apartment. But I'm warning you guys: Bring your own snacks, 'cause you won't find any in our place."

"Fine," I say, though I'm feeling anything but. I have to admit, I'd frame Lillian's sketch of Mr. Mac's ponytail, but I'm not about to let them know it. "Lillian can do the illustrations, and we can all make the dioramas together. Fine."

"Good." Liza smiles. "So that's settled. But what are we actually making? What kinds of food do we eat all the time and think of as 'American' that people would be shocked to find out were brought here by immigrants?"

"Pizza?" Lillian offers. "Most people can't live without pizza. And that came from Italy, obviously."

"Well, if it obviously came from Italy," I say, "no

one will be surprised that it was introduced by immigrants, will they? It's supposed to be a cool, new, surprising fact that the food is from somewhere else."

Lillian and Liza exchange a look. Can I help it if I'm right?

Liza scrunches up her eyes the way she always does when she's thinking hard about something. "What about tacos? I mean, I know they're originally from Mexico, but does everyone know that? We had tacos for lunch again today, and they're all over the place everywhere, right?"

"Lame," I say, not even trying to be nice. "Lame, lame, lame. Everyone knows tacos are from Mexico, or at least some Spanish-speaking place. Haven't you ever seen a Taco Bell commercial?"

Liza looks hurt, and I feel bad. But whatever. Then she crosses her arms and says, "Okay, genius, what's your brilliant idea?"

Good point. I've been so busy concentrating on *how* we would make everything that I haven't actually spent much time thinking about *what* we should make.

"Um, I don't know, exactly. I guess that's what we have to research."

"Yeah," she agrees. "I guess."

Lillian looks up from her sketching. "This may be obvious too, but shouldn't we make some real food? I mean, that's what we're doing in the cooking class, so why don't we take something we learn in there and make *it* a part of the presentation? We can give everyone who visits our exhibit a little taste, like they do in the supermarket. Everyone loves free samples, right?"

Even I have to admit that's a good idea. Liza looks at me, grinning like Nicky does whenever Mom tells him he said something smart. I shrug. "Yeah, I guess. Now we just have to figure out what to make."

We sit there for a minute. Nobody said anything.

The lights flicker, and then the class ends. This is so not going the way I wanted.

# CHAPTER 18
## *Lillian*

All the way to the cooking studio, my mother lectures me about peppers. Who knew that in some countries peppers go by "capsicum," their Latin name? I didn't, but my mother did, along with about a million other random facts about the vegetable—and, by the way, it's actually a *fruit*, if you want to get technical (and, of course, my mother does . . . always). She's telling me all of this because the pepper is today's main ingredient at cooking class, and she wants to make sure I understand that she knows as much about them as Chef Antonio does, probably even more.

While she's going on about all of the different pepper varieties (red! yellow! purple! brown! sweet! tart! spicy!), I search for a radio station that's playing something other than a commercial. We could take the subway to class, but outside of Manhattan, the trains sometimes run slow on the weekends, and my mother hates to wait. She also hates pop music, so I skip over the stations most normal seventh graders would choose and find one that plays country, because that's the only kind of music we can both (sort of) stand to listen to. I think my mother tolerates country songs because they're so melodramatic. A lot of Chinese songs are too—the old-fashioned ones and the popular ones. In parks all over China—and even here in New York City—you'll see people of all ages wailing into the microphone about lost love and other tragedies, just like country-and-western singers do. My mother may not be big on showing her emotions, but she sure has a thing for songs (and soap operas) that are gushing with them.

"It was the Portuguese who brought the chili pepper to Asia," my mother says as she backs carefully into a parking spot near the cooking studio. She shuts off the engine, and the radio goes quiet too, just as the singer was begging his fiancée not to leave. Do people actually pour their hearts out to each other like that in real life? Katie had a boyfriend last year in San Francisco, and I can't imagine him begging her not to move to New York. He didn't have much to say about anything, as far as I could tell, but he did play basketball, get good grades, and have cool hair, which was good enough for Katie, I guess.

"Cayenne peppers are very popular in Szechuan dishes," my mother whispers to me as we rush into the studio. She refuses to be late, and we're not, but most of the class has already arrived: Frankie and her mom, the always-beaming Newlyweds, and Liza, who looks bummed out, despite the fact that Frankie and Mrs. Caputo are clearly trying to make her laugh and have a good time without her mom here. I sneak a glance at the little table in the corner and am disappointed to see that Javier isn't there. My mother is still rattling off facts about peppers under her breath to me—apparently, pepper the spice does not come from pepper the vegetable—and I can't help wishing that Liza and I could magically trade places, at least for the next two hours.

Over at the prep table Chef Antonio is busy pouring ingredients into bowls and arranging everything by recipe. He turns around when he hears us arriving. "Lillian, MeiYin, *buenos días!*" he bellows across the room. It's strange to hear him call my mother by her first name, and even stranger that she doesn't correct him. She always introduces herself as Dr. Wong because of her Ph.D. and calls everyone else Mr. or Mrs. So-and-So. But Chef Antonio likes to keep things informal, and since he's the instructor, I guess my mother has decided it's not her place to correct him. Still, it clearly makes her uncomfortable that everyone in the class (except Liza and Frankie) has been calling her MeiYin like it's no big deal. I probably should feel bad for her, but instead, it makes me smile (secretly) every time.

Errol strolls in, looking so relaxed and good-natured that I'm jealous. Chef ushers us over to a pair of empty stools and takes his place at the head of the table. "Good afternoon, *amigos*, and welcome to the second session of American Cooking 101. Today we will get to know one of my very favorite fruits—or, I should say, fruit families." He opens his arms as if he could wrap them around the entire class. "Like us, they come in many different varieties, each with its own unique and exciting flavor." Chef Antonio reaches under the table, where there must be a hidden shelf, and pulls out a big metal bowl filled with peppers of all different shapes, colors, and sizes. "*Señoras y señores*," he says, taking a round, shiny green pepper in one hand and an orange one in the other, "the *bello* bell pepper." He hands one pepper to Liza on his right and the other to Errol on his left and tells them to take a good look and pass them around. He takes a red pepper from the bowl. It's thinner and pointier than the others and curls up slightly at the end. "The cheeky chili pepper," he says, passing it to Liza. The next one is plump, short, and green. "The heavenly jalapeño."

Chef Antonio goes on like this—the "succulent sweet pepper," the "*bonita* banana pepper"—until the bowl is empty. Ms. Bissessar, my English teacher, would definitely give him an A for alliteration. While we're looking at the peppers, Chef tells us about how, like corn, they're native to the Americas and were spread to other countries by the Europeans after they "discovered" them in the New World. The way he pronounces *conquistadores* sounds like poetry. He explains that some South Asian cultures believe peppers can protect against evil and even bring good luck. As he's talking, my mother nods along like it's her job to confirm that he has his facts straight. Whenever Chef Antonio mentions something that she's already told me—which is often, since she rattled on nonstop during the entire ride to class—my mother nudges me with her elbow, just in case I've forgotten in the past twenty minutes about her vast pepper knowledge.

Chef says we can do anything with peppers—and that includes paprika, which is a kind of dried pepper—because they have so many flavors. Lots of immigrants brought their own pepper practices to America when they came (I make a note of that for our project), and he's chosen a few of his favorites for us to try today. . . .

When it's finally time to start cooking, Liza scoots her stool over to join Frankie and her mom, and I can't help feeling a little jealous. My own mother is holding up the line at the prep table, examining every pepper for the tiniest flaw and probably wishing she'd brought a magnifying glass. I look away from my mother's inspection and watch as Chef Antonio puts his arm around Liza (she must be thrilled!) and steers her over to the empty spot next to Errol. I guess Henry couldn't make it this week either. Liza looks back at Frankie and her mom and then turns and smiles at Errol. The two of them shake hands and laugh, even though they already met last week. Liza's good at talking to people she doesn't really know. If we do end up becoming real friends, someday I'll have to ask her how she does it.

Our first recipe is stuffed peppers. Apparently, stuffed peppers turn up all over the globe—from Spain to India to Scandinavia to Mexico—but we're making a meat-filled Middle Eastern version and a Greek vegetarian version called *yemista*. As usual, my mother is acting like a kitchen czar and assigning me tasks like fetching, measuring, and pouring ingredients, while she does all of the fun stuff—the slicing, the mixing, the stuffing—herself. When Chef comes over to praise our results, my mother doesn't miss the opportunity to mention that she thinks his recipe would taste better with a bit more cardamom and less turmeric.

We put them in the oven and turn to our next dish.

This time we're making pepper jelly, which comes from the American South. I sneak a look over at Liza, since her mom is southern, to see how she's doing. Errol must be pretty entertaining, because she doesn't even seem to notice. Or, at least, if she is still bummed out, she's hiding it well. I guess these savory jellies Chef is talking about are typical all over the South and were originally made to preserve fruits and vegetables for year-round eating. He says people eat it with pickled okra or spread it on shrimp or even fried chicken livers (*That's* why they made pepper jelly—to disguise all the gross stuff they had to eat!).

I'm not sure what I'll think of the taste, but the jelly is really fun to make. We start by "sweating" sweet and jalapeño peppers—which means cooking them until the skins peel off—then crushing red and black peppercorns, bringing it all to a boil, letting the liquid "reduce" and thicken, and then adding something called "pectin" to help it jelly-ize. Some of the steps have to be done at the same time, so my mother has no choice but to let me help. In the few moments when she can't push my hand away and do it herself, there's something really exciting about putting all the ingredients together, transforming them into something different, and then seeing them come out in an entirely new form at the end.

Last up is pepper steak, which Chef Antonio describes as a "Chinese American" dish. Right away my mother rolls her eyes and sighs loudly, letting anyone in a three-block radius know how she feels about Chinese American food. Even when Chef explains that the beef version common in America was originally made with pork in the Chinese province of Fujian—where we actually have relatives—she doesn't seem satisfied, and she shows her annoyance by chopping onions and ginger loudly and ordering me around like even more of a dictator than usual. Our pepper steak is delicious (as is everything we made—even the pepper jelly), but my mother puts down her fork after just one bite and insists that there's nothing Chinese about it. I look over at Liza and Errol, who are eating off the same plate and cracking up like old friends, and wonder what kind of miracle it would take to prevent my mother from coming to class next Saturday.

# CHAPTER 19
## *Liza*

"*Hello*, what is that?" Frankie asks, pointing at the thermos I've just taken out of my lunch bag. "Did you actually bring your lunch? It's a first—we've got to tell Guinness!" She reaches into her backpack and pulls out her phone. "Do you think they text?"

"Ha-ha," I say sarcastically, but I'm smiling for real. It's tuna melt day on the lunch line, and I couldn't be happier that instead of waiting for a cafeteria lady to plop one of those greasy, oozing squares onto my tray, I'm about to dig in to my homemade pepper steak. Believe it or not, Errol let me take home all of our leftovers on Saturday. He said that Henry was so disappointed about having to miss class that Errol promised him they'd cook all of the recipes themselves this week. It's so cool—they were college roommates and just left their jobs (I think Henry was a lawyer and Errol was some kind of money guy) to open the restaurant they've been dreaming about since they were kids. When I told Errol I wasn't in the mood to share anything with Mom after she made me come to class solo, he just shook his head at me and laughed. Then he tipped my chin up, looked me right in the eye, and said, "Young lady, I think you need to cut your mama a break."

I've been replaying what Errol said over and over in my head all week and trying to follow his advice. I know my mom is stressed out about her deadline for the magazine's big issue, and I'm making an effort to be understanding—even though it's not my fault the publisher changed her mind at the last minute. And our class was scheduled first! Okay, so far I probably haven't cut my mom as big of a break as Errol thinks I should, but I've been helping out with Cole more than usual, and I did let Mom have all of the leftover pepper jelly, which we made extra spicy just for her.

Frankie watches me eat my stir-fry a little jealously, even though she has her own lunch right in front of her (it looks like garlic broccoli and chicken Parmesan, a Caputo staple and really tasty). On Saturday she and her mom had a bit more "trouble" with the recipes than the rest of us did, and I'm fairly sure there was nothing to even sample, much less anything to take home.

I stab a hunk of pepper and a slab of steak with my fork and hold it out to Frankie. "Want a bite?" I offer. "You always give me some of yours."

Frankie shakes her head. "That's okay," she says. "It'll just remind me of my mom's latest epic cooking fail. Can you believe that her eye was burning and watering for the rest of the weekend from that fleck of cayenne pepper she managed to flip in there?"

I stifle a giggle. Poor Theresa, these things always happen to her. And believe it or not, it wasn't their only injury. "How's your pinky?" I ask, eyeing Frankie's bandaged little finger.

Frankie rolls her eyes. "It's fine," she says. "Luckily, it was mostly the nail that got nicked."

A paring knife slipped out of Frankie's mom's hand while she was slicing a pepper and landed . . . well, *in* Frankie's. I wonder how things would have gone if I'd tripled up with the Caputos like I'd planned instead of working with Errol. At first I was kind of upset that Chef Antonio asked me to switch—it wasn't like he made me do it, but who could say no to him? In the end, cooking with Errol actually turned out to be pretty fun, and at least I came home with leftovers— and no physical damage.

"Well, I think I'd rather have been in your shoes than Lillian's on Saturday," I say, trying to make

Frankie feel better about the class. "At least your mom doesn't try to out-teach the teacher."

"True." Frankie nods. "I almost felt bad for her." She gives the tables in our section a quick once-over. "So where is Lillian the Librarian today, anyway?"

"Frankie," I say with a sigh, shaking my head. "She skipped lunch to ask Ms. Hernandez for help on last night's math homework. I told her we'd meet up with her in social studies."

The second I mention social studies, Frankie's eyes light up. She must have forgotten that it's Tuesday again. "Well then," she says, quickly packing up her half-eaten chicken parm, "we'd better get going. We don't want to keep Lillian waiting, do we?"

Oh, man. Sometimes Frankie is a real "piece of work," as my dad would say.

We have to stop at our lockers to drop off our lunch bags and grab our notebooks, so by the time we get to Mr. McEnroe's room, the door is already open and people are filing in. I can tell by the way Frankie slams her books on the desk that she's annoyed at having missed out on her usual Tuesday tradition of ogling Mr. Mac before class.

I sit down next to her and then notice Lillian in the back of the room hunched over her math notebook. "Hey, Lillian," I call. "Come sit with us!" She looks up, smiles, and starts to collect her things. Frankie slams another book, and I kick her gently—but firmly—in the shin.

Mr. McEnroe strolls past us on his way to shut the door. "Hello, girls," he says (I can practically feel Frankie melting beside me). "It's great to see how well the three of you are working together."

Frankie shoots Mr. Mac a smile that says, *Well, what did you expect?* while Lillian and I exchange a look and roll our eyes. I mean, I hope Lillian hasn't picked up on the extent of Frankie's snarkiness, but no way has she missed it entirely.

Mr. McEnroe makes his way to the front of the room. "I have some exciting news to share today. At least I think it's exciting, and I hope you will too."

Frankie nods vigorously in agreement, even though she has no idea what he's talking about.

"I've decided to add another component to our Immigration Museum project," Mr. Mac continues. "Since we'll be inviting all of your parents to join us, I thought it might be fun to give them an assignment of their own. To make things even more festive and inclusive, I'm going to ask your parents to bring in a dish representative of their cultural heritage for everyone to share. We can call the whole event 'Museum Night'!"

I look at Frankie and know what she's thinking: Thank goodness her dad knows how to make some amazing Italian food, because her mom is definitely not going to be allowed anywhere near the kitchen for this assignment.

Lillian is probably worrying that whatever traditional dish her mother decides to make will be so elaborate, it will outshine our own project.

And me? I'm wondering where my mom will find the time to whip up anything more "homemade" than microwave popcorn. I make a note in my homework folder to call my dad tonight. It would be so cool if he could come.

# CHAPTER 20
## *Frankie*

"DUDE, you are so dead!"

Man . . . that's just great. Goons. Here I am bringing Liza and Lillian over to start making some of the pieces of our project, and what are we greeted with as we enter the house but the unmistakable sound of thundering Goons. I motion for Liza and Lillian to come on in behind me. "Watch it, guys, I'm afraid we're not alone. Keep your eyes open for projectiles and your heads down."

They both laugh like I'm kidding. I am *so* not.

We put our stuff down in the hallway as far as possible from the monstrous pile of backpacks and skateboards that, unfortunately, means everybody is home. I just can't win. I lead Liza and Lillian straight to the kitchen because there's no point in confronting the enemy on an empty stomach.

Oh, goodie, Dad and Nicky are already there. Deep breaths. Dad's presence can sometimes keep things under control.

They seem to be making something in a blender— very loudly.

"Hi, Dad," I start over the noise, but Nicky has seen us already and, squealing with excitement, rushes over to Liza, one of his favorite people in the world. He launches into the plot of a comic book about Greek gods that he's reading. Not only does he love the Greek gods, he totally believes in them, and somewhere along the way he decided that Liza did too. She's super nice to him, way nicer than I am.

"Um, hi, Dad," I say again. Still nothing. "DAD!" He shuts off the blender and turns around.

"Hello, ladies!" He's really charming, my dad, so that sounds less dorky than you'd think. "So nice to see you, Liza, and what's your name, kiddo?" I introduce him to Lillian, right away to avoid another lecture from Liza about being rude.

"Hi, Mr. Caputo," they both say together, and then giggle. It's not that funny.

"Dad, remember how I said last night that we were coming here to work on our project? We just want to get a little food and start working."

"Sure thing, hon, sure thing. We had a ton of super-ripe fruit, so it seemed like a good day for smoothies. Help yourselves. And the avocados were turning, so I made some guacamole earlier. Grab those corn chips on the counter and dig in. Your brothers already blew through here, which is why I hid a pitcher of the smoothies. They should clear out of your hair soon. I think I heard them hunting down their gear for soccer practice."

He starts piling up assorted dishes and cleaning the kitchen. My dad likes his domain to be "ship-shape," as he says.

Just then we hear another crash overhead, and this time the kitchen literally shakes. Liza and Lillian look around, probably wondering if we need to crawl under a table or something.

"Sorry, guys, that's just The Goons in motion. Let's grab some food and spread out at the dining room table. If we're lucky, they'll be out of here soon."

While Nicky is still telling elaborate tales about Apollo and Hephaestus that nobody in their right mind could follow, I get our snacks together. Liza and Lillian are too nice to blow Nicky off, so I intervene. "Nicky! Cut it out. Right now! Nobody wants to hear it, okay?"

For a minute he just stares at me, and I think I can see tears in his eyes. I actually start to feel bad, but then he looks at Liza, who gives him one of her biggest smiles. "Liza does." Then he points to Lillian, who still appears to be listening to his nonsense too. "I like your new friend better than YOU, Frankie!"

Now that I have everything on a tray, I lead the way to the other room. "I can live with that."

They help me push aside all the papers, folders, notices, mail, clean socks, and other stuff that collects, like dust, on our dining room table. I have no idea where it all comes from or how the six of us manage to eat here every day. I remember the serenity of Lillian's house, and I'm more than a little embarrassed.

"Sorry about that," I say as I put out the snacks. "Nicky loves an audience."

Liza turns back to pull the pocket doors closed behind us. "Totally okay, Franks. You know I think he's cute. At least he speaks in full sentences, which is more than I can say for my brother!"

Lillian steps on a LEGO and looks startled.

"Sorry, Lillian," I tell her. "One of the hazards of Casa Caputo."

"No, no, it's fine," she says, carefully picking up the LEGO and setting it on a shelf. "I just don't want to break anything."

"Oh, please," I laugh. "Like they'd ever notice . . ." We attack the bowl of chips and guac and slurp down the smoothies. My dad definitely has a talent for whipping up something delicious out of whatever we happen to have around. Chances are he discovered the fruit in our smoothies buried under a pile of papers and minutes away from rotting, which is what inspired him to make them in the first place. No need to share my suspicions with Liza and Lillian, though.

Just as we're about to finally get down to work, the floor throbs and the pocket doors slam back into the walls. The Goons have arrived.

"Hey, girls! And Frankie! Whatcha doing?" Leo, my oldest brother, booms. He booms everything he says. He's permanently booming—Mom says he has no volume control. Joey just grins and ransacks the place, like a really moronic robber.

"Ha-ha. What do you guys want? Dad promised you were out of here."

"What? And leave you girls here alone and defenseless? Francesca, how could you suggest such a thing?" Leo snickers again and then socks Joey in the arm. "DUDE, what did you do with the schedule? AM I going to have to kill you?"

I notice that Liza is looking at him with a certain expression—and I recognize it. No way. No way does she think he's cute. Impossible. I won't allow it. Lillian, on the other hand, looks stunned, as though aliens have just landed in my dining room. Now, *that* is a normal reaction.

"Why don't you check the pocket in the master calendar?" I say, not caring if I sound like the know-it-all they say I am. "Isn't that where all that stuff is supposed to go so Mom and Dad can keep track of it?"

Leo scratches his head like a cartoon character,

making himself look even dumber than usual. "Duh, Frankie, why didn't we think of that? 'CAUSE IT'S NOT THERE, genius!"

Joey pulls a tattered sheet of paper from under the mail, waving it around like he's found the golden ticket. "Got it!"

Leo pumps his fist. "Yes!" He grabs his bag and then nods in our direction. "Later, gators. We're out!"

And then they're gone, as quickly as they came. Like the tornado in *The Wizard of Oz.*

I shake my head. "They are so repulsive," I say, and get up to close the doors again. "Now, where were we?"

"Frankie, you're so hard on your brothers," Liza says. "All of them. I mean, they're not that bad. And at least it's never dull around here."

Even Lillian agrees. "I thought your brothers were funny. My sister is so *not* funny. Or fun. She's just perfect, which can get really boring to be around."

I give this some thought. For about half a second.

"Perfect *and* boring? I'll take it. My brothers are a nonstop disaster waiting to happen. You can try to be prepared, but it's never what you think. I spent practically the whole day on Sunday trying to get melted wax out of my clothes because some genius— who wasn't necessarily Nicky—left a crayon in his pocket that went through the laundry and melted all over the place. There were purple streaks on everything! And the whole time I was scrubbing my clothes with some nasty toxic 'miracle' cleaner, all I did was wish I were an only child. But a perfect sister sounds pretty good too. Perfect sisters don't destroy everything in their path. Caputo Goons and Goon wannabes, on the other hand, do major damage before breakfast. Without even trying."

Instead of feeling bad for me, Liza and Lillian are laughing their heads off. Silly me, expecting sympathy.

"Thanks for the support," I say. *Geez.*

When they finally get a hold of themselves, we actually do get down to work and start to tackle the details of our project, like plotting out the dioramas and making supply lists. The best diorama, I think, will be the one about bagels. Everyone loves bagels, right? But does everyone know who brought them to America? I seriously doubt it. They were brought here by Eastern Europeans, Jews mostly, and sold on food carts in big cities. Why the holes? So they could be stacked up on poles attached to the carts, and when a customer wanted one, all the seller had to do was slide it off. Our diorama will have tiny little bagels being sold by tiny little peddlers in tiny little caps, in the middle of a crowded street scene from the turn of the last century. Thinking about how this is actually beginning to shape up into a real project, I start to feel better. "Awesome" is starting to seem possible, and I don't plan on handing in anything less than awesome to Mr. Mac.

We're deciding what to make for the other dioramas when there's a loud explosion in the kitchen. All three of us jump out of our seats to see what's going on and discover that Nicky has decided to make a smoothie for my mom when she gets home, only he forgot to put the top on the blender. Pink globs of cold, sticky smoothie splatter us the second we open the door, and big goopy drops plop onto our heads from the ceiling.

So much for project planning. Liza and Lillian take off to wash the pink slime from their hair. They're laughing as they go, but I don't see what's funny. Maybe one of The Goons should have just killed me when we walked in. At least that would have put me out of my misery.

# CHAPTER 21
## *Lillian*

If there's one food you can be sure never to find in our refrigerator, it's cheese. There is nothing Chinese about cheese, and even though my parents have lived in America almost as long as they lived in China, they've just never "developed a taste for it," as Chef Antonio would say. I, on the other hand, *love* cheese. One of my favorite things about moving to Brooklyn is going to the old Italian grocery stores on Saturday mornings and buying fresh-made mozzarella. If you order it salted—which you should—the guy behind the counter scoops up a big blob of it with his giant tongs and dips it into a vat of salty water before stuffing it into a container and topping it with an extra splash of salt water for good measure. The cheese is so fresh, the container warms your hands, and it's almost impossible not to stick your fingers in and tear off a piece before you even leave the store.

Why am I going on about cheese? Because it's the theme of today's cooking class, which means my mother is acting even snootier than usual. Unlike last week, when she turned into a living, breathing Wikipedia page about peppers, my mother hasn't tried to wow the class with even a single fact about cheese today. Instead, while Chef is telling us that people have been making cheese for ten thousand years and that it's mentioned in Greek mythology (Nicky would be excited!) and pictured in hieroglyphics on ancient Egyptian tombs (cool!), she's got her arms crossed over her chest and a bored expression on her face. Whatever. Since Mama seems completely uninterested in cheese, maybe I'll actually get to do some of the cooking today, instead of just helping her do it.

Just as Chef Antonio is about to introduce our first recipe, the door to the studio slams open noisily and in come Liza and her mom. They've got Liza's little brother, Cole, with them too, and he doesn't seem very happy about the way Liza's mom used his stroller to shove the door open. I'm relieved Liza made it—I was starting to worry—but her mom looks stressed out as usual, and I'm pretty sure they hadn't planned on bringing Cole again.

Chef rushes over and holds the door open for Ms. Reynolds and the stroller. "I am so sorry," she says, spinning around to pick up the Matchbox car Cole just threw on the floor. "His ear's been bothering him, and I think he's getting another tooth . . . The sitter actually showed up, but at the last minute I just couldn't leave him."

I make eye contact with Liza, who isn't smiling. She rolls her eyes.

*"Por favor,"* says Chef Antonio as he squats down to Cole's level and hands him the car, "no apologies." He stands and looks at Liza's mom. "And no more babysitters. Your little boy is welcome to come here every week—my mother would like nothing better." Chef gestures to the corner of the studio where Javier is slumped over his phone like always and Angelica is sitting in a window seat doing some kind of intricate needlework. When she sees Cole, she jumps up and claps her hands together, her perfectly penciled lips spreading into a wide smile.

Liza's mom unbuckles Cole's stroller straps, and Angelica immediately swoops him up into her arms. He coos and hands her the Matchbox car, which she pretends to drive up one of his arms and down the other.

"That's very sweet of you," Liza's mom says as Cole practically bubbles over in giggles. "But too generous. He can be a real handful."

"*Este chiquito?*" Angelica says, leaning in to rub noses with Cole. "A handful of fun maybe! Right, *papi*?"

Cole grabs two chubby fistfuls of Angelica's curls and hollers, "More, more, more!"

Liza's mom looks horrified and is about to yank his hands away when Angelica makes it clear she doesn't mind by giving Cole another nose rub and dancing him over to the window to look out at all the real cars. Liza looks relieved and, grabbing her mom's hand, pulls her over to the big table, where the rest of us are trying to act like we haven't been staring at them, transfixed by their family drama. Good thing I remembered to turn off the video camera.

"Okay!" Chef Antonio bellows, clapping his hands. "The gang's all here!" Embarrassed, Liza and her mom wave sheepishly at everyone. "Now," Chef says, "where was I? Oh yes—my favorite question: How did people first discover that milk can become cheese? Does anyone know?"

Immediately, all eyes are on my mother, who, until now, has blurted out an answer to every one of Chef's questions practically before he's even finished asking them. Mama raises her eyebrows, clearly taken aback. Apparently, the origin of cheese is not among her areas of culinary expertise.

"How about someone other than MeiYin?" Chef quickly asks, saving the day. Relieved, my mother lets out a tiny, nervous laugh before the superior expression settles over her face again.

Mrs. Newlywed raises her hand halfway. She doesn't usually say much, so, of course, everyone's curious to hear her answer. I point my camera in her direction and start taping.

"Um, this might sound disgusting, but if I remember correctly, a long time ago traders or herdsmen or people like that stored milk in animal stomachs— which contain the rennet that you need to turn milk into cheese. So, at some point, someone was carrying milk in a cow or sheep stomach, and when they went to pour it out, well, it wasn't milk anymore."

Liza and Frankie both look as grossed out as I feel. Everyone else looks impressed, including my mother, even though I can tell she's trying not to let it show.

"*Perfecto!*" Chef Antonio booms, and gives Mrs. Newlywed a hearty round of applause.

Mr. Newlywed looks surprised, as if he's just discovered something new and fascinating about his wife. "What?" she says, giving him a playful shove. "I took food science as an undergrad."

"So," Chef says, "now that we know how milk becomes cheese, we're going to make some cheese of our own. On the prep table behind me is a sheep stomach for everyone—"

"Ew!" Liza, Frankie, and I scream in accidental unison. A few others around the table gasp in disgust. Even Javier looks up from his phone.

"Gotcha!" the chef cries, pointing at us. "Lucky for us, there are other ways to make cheese. No stomachs required—except for eating."

We all laugh, including Javier. I realize I'm aiming the camera at him and quickly turn it off. My cheeks get hot and I hope he doesn't notice.

Our first recipe is for an Indian cheese called *paneer*, which is really fun to make. You have to heat the milk until it almost boils and then add lemon juice, causing it to form these funny little clumps called "curds." Then you strain the curds through a cheesecloth, wrap them up, and squeeze out all of the liquid.

Even though cheese isn't her thing, my mother turns back into her bossy self and orders me around as usual. Only this time she's just talking, because she actually lets me do almost everything. I'm surprised, but I don't want to ruin it by asking why, so I just do what Mr. McEnroe always tells us to and "go with the flow."

You can't use *paneer* right away, so while ours chills in a bowl of ice water, Chef Antonio gives us each a bowlful from a batch that he made yesterday, and we stir up a spicy spinach and pea stew to pour on top of it. As soon as the ingredients switch from cheese curds to vegetables and curry, my mother takes over again and it's back to slicing and dicing for me. I don't mind, though, because there are still two recipes to go, and I've finally discovered her weakness. If my mother were Superman, cheese would be her Kryptonite. Call me Lex Luthor, but I'm definitely enjoying catching a glimpse of her "mere mortal" side for a change.

# CHAPTER 22
## *Liza*

"I know there's one around here somewhere," I tell Frankie and Lillian. I'm standing on the kitchen counter in my socks and searching the cabinets for this fondue set that was originally my grandmother's, I think. Ever since we made cheese fondue in cooking class on Saturday, we've all been haunted by the delicious lava of melted cheese, and we decided to do our project planning over here this afternoon so we could make some while we work.

Frankie pops up from behind the refrigerator door holding a half-empty package of my brother's cheese sticks. "This was the only thing I could find that even resembles cheese," she says, eyeing it, "and I'm not even sure it qualifies."

Frankie's used to the sorry state of our fridge, so I'm not embarrassed for her to see it anymore. Lillian, on the other hand, is staring at the bare shelves like an archaeologist uncovering a rare artifact for the first time. "Why don't I run out and get some, um, more cheese?" she suggests. "You know, like the kind we used in class."

Chef Antonio's recipe calls for a combination of Swiss and Gruyère, but he said cheddar or any other kind of good melting cheese works just as well. "Good idea," I say, still poking around for the fondue pot. "Better check to see if we have the other ingredients first."

Amazingly, Frankie discovers that we actually have enough flour and butter for the fondue, but we need bread and some fruit for dipping. "We should get something to drink, too," says Frankie as she closes the refrigerator door. "All I saw in there were juice boxes."

"Got it," Lillian agrees, not looking up from her shopping list. Instead of words, she's drawn tiny detailed pictures of everything we need. From up here, I can see that Frankie's watching her too, and I can tell she's as fascinated as I am.

"Why don't you go with her, Franks?" Maybe the two of them going on a mission to the grocery store without me would help Frankie get over her thing with Lillian. Frankie shoots me a raised-eyebrow look that I'm glad Lillian's too focused on her list to notice. So much for that idea.

"I think I'd better stay here and help you find the fondue set," Frankie says. "You don't mind going solo, do you, Lillian?"

"Not at all," says Lillian, grabbing her list and heading for the door. I give her some money from the grocery jar Mom keeps in the cabinet above the stove. I guess Lillian didn't want to be alone with Frankie either.

I step over the stove to get to the very last of the cabinets, a small one just two shelves high that's above the refrigerator. It's almost impossible to reach unless you're doing what I'm doing now, and my mom definitely would not approve. Our apartment may look a little empty and neglected, but my mother is religious about keeping it clean—and feet on the countertops totally wouldn't fly.

"Found it!" I call down to Frankie, who, instead of helping me search for the fondue set, has been studying the perfect miniature bagels and hot dogs (two foods we're pretty sure everyone will be surprised to learn came from immigrant cultures) that Lillian has made out of modeling clay. Frankie stuffs the tiny replicas back into their sandwich bag when she sees that I've caught her admiring Lillian's work.

The fondue set is still in its original box. On one

side is a diagram of everything that's supposed to be inside—the fondue pot, the stand it sits in, the heater, and six metal skewers that have fancy little hoops on the end you're supposed to hold. On the other side of the box is a picture of some people at a party, holding their drinks in one hand and dipping their skewers of sliced apple or cubes of bread into the pot of bright orange cheese with the other. All of the colors are overly bright, or "saturated," as Hank—our sixth-grade digital media teacher, who insisted we call him by his first name—used to say. Frankie and I both have an app on our phones that can make any picture you take look like a relic from the 1970s, just like the one on this box.

I climb down from the counter and set the box on what my mom calls the "breakfast bar," which is really just a slab of wood that sticks out from a low wall behind the sink. Below it are three stools where you can sit and see right into the kitchen and chat with whoever is cooking. I used to love to climb up onto one of the stools and watch my mom peeling vegetables or mixing up pie dough. Sometimes she'd give me something simple to do, like snapping the stems off string beans or sprinkling flour onto a sheet of wax paper. Other times I was happy just to watch her work and tell her about going to the playground with Sonya or building an igloo with Frankie or whatever else I'd done that day. Now we use the breakfast bar mostly for piling up catalogs that no one ever gets around to reading and the scribbles and finger paintings Cole brings home practically every day that my mom can never bring herself to throw away.

"I can't stop staring at this picture," Frankie says as I take the fondue pot and its accessories out of the box. "Everyone just looks so 'groovy,' don't you think?" The women in the photo all have those big '70s hairdos that poof out at the top and flip up at the ends. Several of the men have mustaches and long sideburns. They're all smiling and showing a lot of teeth, except for one couple who are feeding each other strawberries dipped in chocolate. I try to imagine my grandparents at a party like the one on the box, but it's hard. For one thing, one set of grandparents is black, and since everyone in the picture is white, I'm pretty sure they wouldn't have been invited.

The doorbell rings, and I buzz Lillian in while Frankie tears herself away from the groovy picture to get the fondue going on the stove. Before you actually add any cheese, you start with something called a "roux," which Chef showed us how to make by melting butter over low heat and then stirring in flour until it's thick and smooth. Lillian and I cut up small cubes of the cheese she bought, plunk them into the simmering roux, and watch them melt.

"Hey," Lillian says, "what about the wine?" In class we'd added white wine to our fondue, which Chef Antonio assured our mothers was okay because the alcohol burns off from the heat. Still, Lillian's mother didn't like the idea of cooking with wine around us "kids," and she insisted on leaving it out of their version. I think her plan sort of backfired, though, because Lillian went around tasting everyone else's fondue to see what she was missing.

Frankie and I exchange a look. *Is she serious?* I'm about to ask, when Lillian suddenly bursts out laughing. "Gotcha!"

All three of us crack up—even Frankie. Maybe, just maybe, her ice queen act with Lillian is starting to melt a little, like the hunks of cheese in our fondue.

We turn off the stove and pour our wineless concoction into my grandmother's fondue pot. Since we can't figure out how to light the heater, we decide to skip it and make it our goal to finish off the fondue before it cools and hardens. There's not enough room on the breakfast bar for a proper fondue experience, so we place the pot in the middle of the dining room table, shoving aside our notebooks and the beginnings of our dioramas. Frankie brings over a tray of apples and pears that she's cut into cubes, and I quickly slice the baguette that Lillian bought and toss the pieces into a bowl. We each take one of the skewers, spear a hunk of fruit or bread, and try to look sophisticated as we dip it into the fondue and then into our mouths.

*Yum.*

We've just finished doing our best impressions of the groovy people on the box and started painting and gluing our diorama pieces in place when the front door swings open and my mom and Cole come in. Frankie, Lillian, and I look at one another. Is it really six o'clock? Not only have we barely begun our work, but we've left a massive mess of melted cheese, apple cores, bread crumbs, and papier-mâché all over the kitchen and dining room. My mom smiles at Frankie and Lillian, but she doesn't look pleased.

"I see you girls are feeling creative," she says, picking a fondue skewer wrapped in a gloppy strip of newspaper off the floor. When her nostrils begin to flare, just a little, all three of us start packing everything up and whisking plates and bowls to the sink as quickly as we can. Only we're not fast enough to stop my brother from grabbing a fistful of bread and dunking practically his whole arm into what's left of the fondue. Good thing we didn't use the heater, or Cole would have been covered with blisters in addition to cheese.

"I should probably go," says Lillian, after we've managed to tame the mess somewhat. She shoves her notebooks into her backpack and carefully tucks the bag of miniature food for our project into her jacket pocket. "Thanks for letting us use your fondue set, Ms. Reynolds," she calls after my mom, who's dragging Cole to the bathroom while trying to keep him from touching anything with his cheesy hand.

"Wait up," Frankie says as Lillian heads for the door.

Lillian looks at me, but all I can do is shrug. She turns to Frankie. "Me?"

"Sure," Frankie says. "I'll, um, walk out with you."

I don't know what Frankie's up to, but when she

turns to wave good-bye, I mouth the words *Be nice* and give her my best "I mean business" look.

*Who me?* Frankie mouths back, and raises her eyebrow at me, as usual. "Bye, Ms. Reynolds. Stay cheesy Cole!"

I clean up the rest of the mess so that by the time Cole's in his pj's and Mom's in her sweats, everything is back to normal. I find a space for the fondue set in a lower cabinet, though, so it'll be easier to get to the next time we're feeling groovy.

# CHAPTER 23

*Frankie*

I loathe being late, but we usually are, no matter how many notices I post on the Caputo family calendar. It's supposed to be the master organizer—one glance and my parents know where each of us has to be at all times. Of course, that only works when they actually look at it or pay enough attention to it to remember what it says. And since that only happens about 20 percent of the time, we end up running late the other 80.

The only reason my mom and I had been making it to the cooking classes on time was that I lied to her about when they started. Unfortunately, she chatted with Liza's mom on the way out last week and is now in possession of the correct information. Communication between moms never bodes well. Plus, Liza and her mom were making us look good by straggling in behind us, thanks to Cole, but now that they're bringing him to hang out with the most glam grandma I've ever seen, even they have started beating us to class.

We barrel in, and my mom starts telling her wacky stories of this morning's misadventures: Nicky sticking a fork into the toaster (he's totally fine!); meeting our neighbor, old Mr. Vallo, and his equally ancient dog; The Goons "borrowing" her debit card. Does she always have to be so . . . so . . . her?

We take our seats, with not as much dignity as I would like, and the class can officially start. I tell myself not to have hopes for today, since Mom has pretty much destroyed everything we've done in class so far and, as The Goons keep reminding me, she has not improved *at all*. I mean, not even the tiniest bit. Today's theme is pasta, so you might think she's got this one sewn up. Think again. I decide that low expectations are the best defense.

Chef Antonio beams at us. "Bueno, bueno, amigos, we can start!" He has large, graceful hands that he likes to rub together when he's excited—which seems to be most of the time.

"Today we launch into pasta, or 'noodles,' some people say," He looks over at Cole, giggling with Angelica the Baby Tamer. Javier is there too, and I can tell he's only half listening to his iPod and half to his dad. Not that he'd admit it, of course, which I totally get.

"Most of you may know that pasta originated in China, not Italy. A few years ago a four-thousand-year-old bowl of pasta was discovered buried near China's Yellow River. Probably not too tasty now, but pretty amazing, *qué?* This pasta was made from millet, but it shows that chefs everywhere owe *muchas gracias* to the Chinese, once again. For who could live without pasta today? And since pasta can be dried, it is something you could probably eat forever!"

Chef grins at Lillian's mom, who gives him a thin-lipped smile—of approval, I think, but it's hard to tell with her.

"We know that pasta made its way across the world with no help from Marco Polo, in spite of the myth. It migrated through traders to North Africa, then Arab traders brought it to Sicily. The Italians made it their own by adding durum wheat for binding and by creating pasta in every shape imaginable. It spread through Europe from there, and everybody found a use for it."

Chef Antonio holds up a poster showing at least one hundred different shapes of pasta—twists, tubes, loops, even stars—and I check to make sure Lillian is videotaping. (She is—if there's one positive thing I can say about her, Lillian is definitely proving herself to be reliable.)

"There are literally thousands of shapes, thousands! *Dios mío!* And the Europeans brought many of them here to America. But pasta took a while to catch on. Your Thomas Jefferson had some kind of cheese macaroni in France and then served it at the White House, but nobody liked it. Then, when all the Italians came later and planted the proper kind of wheat, well, Americans have not stopped eating it since!"

He looks around, like we should all be as thrilled with this news as he is. And I am—I mean, pasta. My entire family would probably starve without it.

Chef points us to the workstations he's set up. "It was very challenging to narrow down what we could make today. I wanted you to see the universe of possibilities! But it had to be done, so I made some tough, but tasty, choices!"

We head over to the prep area, to survey what we will be making. I see a mound of what looks like mashed potatoes and chopped onion, a sheet of fresh pasta dough, more pasta of a different color, eggs, and little rice-shaped pasta.

Chef sweeps his arm grandly over the whole room. "Surprise! No Italian pasta. Too easy, too expected! Instead, we make potato pierogi from Poland, we make orzo from Greece, and we make longevity noodles from pasta's mother country, China. When you eat them, they should bring you a long life. And what could be *mejor* than that?"

Lillian's mom makes a little noise, like a chirp, and I can see that she is most definitely pleased. Well, well, who knew?

Liza's mom, who seems more relaxed here than I've seen her in a long time, puts her hand on her hip. "Well, I can tell you that my former Jewish mother-in-law would be disappointed. Her noodle kugel is just about the best thing I ever put in my mouth." Um, what's going on here? She sounds like she's complaining, but she has a sly smile on her face.

Liza seems pleased that her mom is joining in, but a little confused at the same time. We lock eyes for a moment, and mine tell her: *It's all good, whatever it is, it's all good.*

There's a chorus of other pasta demands from everybody else. Chef ducks his head, laughing. "*Amigos, amigos,* we could spend weeks on noodles alone, and if you want to—*bueno*—let's make another class! But for now, how do you say: Don't kill the messenger? I did the best I could!"

Liza's mom is still smiling, and Chef Antonio doesn't take his eyes off her. She smooths the white chef's apron we all wear and says, "Well, I have a mind to just bring Nana's kugel in next time, and you, sir, will never think about noodles the same way again."

Everybody chuckles, and I notice Henry giving Liza a playful punch in the arm. She starts telling him about her nana's cooking, like she's known him all her life. How does she do that? They keep chatting while we all turn to our workstations.

Mom and I start on the pierogi first. We're supposed to roll out the dough, then cut shapes with a drinking glass, and then plop a spoonful of what turns out to be mashed potato, cheese, and onion into the middle. We have to fold the circle closed and then crimp the edges a bit. Sounds fun, right?

A boiling vat of water waits on the stove for these babies when we finish. My mom looks at the materials and grimaces at me. "Well, Franks, let's jump in. Wish we were just opening a box of pasta and dumping it into the water."

Yeah, right, like she does so well at that.

We do okay rolling out the dough—apparently, there's sour cream in it to make it creamier and stickier. I turn the glass upside down and churn out a bunch of circles—so far so good. But when we get to the stuffing-them stage, things get a little uglier. Sometimes we plop in too much mashed potato stuff, other times not enough, and our little guys don't want to stay shut. We try dropping one in the water, and it pops open right away, so that the pasta floats on the surface like a dead moth and the potato nugget sinks to the bottom.

Chef Antonio comes over—to the rescue, I hope. "*Chicas*, what are we doing here?" He shows us a better potato-to-pasta ratio, but our pierogi still wind up looking like uneven, slightly sickly nuggets, not the gleaming, appealingly chubby ones that other people are making. I'm a little relieved to see that both the Newlyweds and Henry and Errol are having some trouble, although not as much as we are.

Looking over at Lillian and her mom, who are very quiet today, my heart sinks. Whoa, I have to admit, Lillian's pierogi are beautiful. I notice that she's the one shaping them, rather than her mother. That's unusual. Her mom seems less comfortable with the rolling pin and has moved on to sautéing onions for the topping. But Lillian? Her hands are quick and precise, and she is making perfect dumplings.

It doesn't look like she's been shooting much video today, though.

Our onions are also cooking, but my mom's eyes are streaming from chopping them, and it gets worse every time she stirs the pan. So she doesn't. Stir them, that is. Our onions blacken, which seems ideal for our hard little pierogi nuggets.

Next up: Longevity noodles, or *chang shou mian*, as Lillian's mom tells us (at least three times). This seems a little easier. Mom is relieved.

"Now we're talking, right, Frankie? Pedal to the metal, as Dad likes to say."

We cook the egg noodles just fine and set them aside. Then we heat up some chicken broth, soy sauce, sesame oil, spices, and cornstarch (okay, that lumps up a bit, but whatever—nobody's perfect). Then we crack the egg over the hot soupy stuff, trying to make it ooze through the tines of a fork, like Chef is showing us.

"Whisk, *chicas*," he urges, "whisk."

Instead of making thin little strands in the broth like everyone else's, ours clumps. We pour the soup over the noodles. Uh-oh, looks like we skipped the step of rinsing and separating the pasta. Great, our long-life soup is a steaming, tangled-up mess. This can't be good luck.

But when we get to the orzo, we do better. We just boil the little ricelike pasta, then chop up peppers (our old friends!), olives, and capers, crumble some sour feta cheese, mix up some lemon juice, vinegar, olive oil, and spices and stir it all up in a bowl. The less actual cooking the better, apparently. I look around the room. Our dish looks as presentable as anyone else's! As everyone brings their food to the large table so we can all eat together, I turn around to high-five my mom. This stuff isn't easy for her, and she really does try hard.

Oops! I guess I spoke too soon. Mom was just supposed to be turning off our burner on the large, communal stove. But instead, she's holding a flaming pot holder and racing for the sink. People are looking up from either wrapping up their cooking or starting to eat, and then they're half laughing, half shrieking. Javier has come over to the table to eat, along with Cole and Angelica—so we have quite the audience. Lillian's mom just looks horrified.

Oh well. For a minute there, just a minute, we seemed almost normal.

# CHAPTER 24
## *Lillian*

I'm dreaming about hanging out in Golden Gate Park with Sierra when the smell of fresh *you tiao* wakes me up. It was a good dream—Sierra and I were playing Frisbee with her dog, GoGo (*gǒu* is the Chinese word for "dog"), who's sort of like my stepdog (or was, I guess) since Katie is allergic and my parents will never let us get one. Thinking about Sierra and GoGo makes me homesick all over again, but it's hard to feel totally depressed when there's *you tiao* waiting downstairs.

In China *you tiao* is a street food that you buy from a cart on the way to work or school, but it's hard to find in America—even in some Chinatowns—so my mother makes her own. The literal translation of *you tiao* is "oil stick," which doesn't exactly sound appetizing. But they're actually long, thin pieces of fried dough, like a straightened-out doughnut or a Mexican churro. My mother turns up her nose at them, like she does at almost anything fun, but my father, Katie, and I could eat them all day. There's nothing like a fresh *you tiao*—hot and greasy in your hand, then crisp, doughy, and sweet on your tongue—to chase away the blues on a Sunday morning.

I race down the stairs.

In the kitchen my mother hovers over the stove with tongs in hand, waiting until the dough has been sizzling in the oil just long enough to achieve the perfect balance of crispiness on the outside and melt-in-your-mouth softness on the inside before plucking it from the pot and laying it on the paper towels that are waiting on the counter to sop up the extra grease. At the table my father is hidden behind a Chinese newspaper and Katie leans over one of her massive textbooks, ignoring the untouched slice of melon on her plate. They're both drinking coffee, one of the few American habits my father has picked up in the twenty years he's lived in the States. Whenever I remind him of it (like when he's going on about how inefficient the subway system in New York is compared to other big cities like Beijing or Shanghai), he says there are Starbucks all over China now too, as if that's some kind of stamp of approval for his liking the nontraditional Chinese beverage.

My mother transfers the *you tiao* to a plate and carries it over to the table. My father and I don't even give her a chance to set it down before we each grab a steaming hot *you tiao* and drop it on our own plate, sticking our burning fingers in our mouths to cool them down and sucking off the fresh grease. I take a bite of mine and close my eyes so I can fully appreciate the flavor. When I open them again, my mother is about to put a *you tiao* on Katie's plate, but Katie waves it away.

"Don't you want one?" I ask, holding mine up. "They're really yummy."

Katie shakes her head firmly. "Too greasy. Do you know how many calories those things have? Or what they'll do to your complexion?"

"Who cares?" I shrug. "Since when do you worry about that stuff? You're a stick and you've never had a pimple in your life."

"Maybe not yet, but I'll become a pizza-faced pig if I keep eating stuff like that. And so will you."

My mother drops her tongs loudly onto the counter, instantly getting our attention (not my father's, though—he's back to his newspaper and probably hasn't heard a word we've said).

"*Nü'ér,*" she says, which means "daughter," and she only calls one of us that when she wants to remind us how low our branch is on the family tree, "I made that food with my two hands and the very best ingredients. You may choose not to eat it, but you must not be disrespectful. A simple 'no thank you' will do."

Katie looks down at the table. "I'm sorry, Mama." She turns to me with an expression that she could have stolen right from Frankie's face. "*No thank you*, Lillian, I would not like a *you tiao*," she says in an overly polite, sarcastic way. Katie and I aren't exactly best friends, but she's not usually outright mean either.

My mother abandons her pot of boiling oil and comes back to the table. She closes Katie's book and pushes her plate in front of her. "Eat your melon, Wei Wei," she says. "Nobody goes hungry in this house."

Katie rolls her eyes, then picks up her melon and takes a bite. "I'll take it to go," she says, getting up and grabbing her book with her free hand. "I've got to go upstairs and study."

"Big test," my mother says when Katie has gone. Shocking. My sister goes to a high school for serious brains where they have a "big test" practically every day. It sounds like torture to me, but Katie lives for that stuff. She says she "thrives under pressure," but if studying on Sunday morning and choosing melon over *you tiao* is thriving, I think I'll stick to just getting by.

"I'll have hers, then," I say, taking a second greasy stick of fried dough and savoring every bite. I know I'm lucky that I don't have to worry about what I eat. At least not yet, anyway. I can't imagine stressing about gaining weight every time I eat French fries or ice cream or my mother's delicious fried dumplings. I hope when I'm fifteen, I'll still appreciate a fresh *you tiao* instead of obsessing over how fattening it is or how it could ruin my perfect skin.

My mother takes off her apron and hangs it on the magnetic hook on the side of the refrigerator. "I'm going to the market," she says. "I was thinking of making *chang shou mian* tonight."

She picks up a sheet of paper from the counter. It's the recipe for the long-life noodles we made in cooking class yesterday. Hmm. Is my mother—MeiYin Wong, the Queen of Chinese Cuisine—actually going to follow one of Chef Antonio's recipes?

"What's that, Mama?" I ask innocently, pointing at the sheet of paper.

She folds the paper in half and slips it into her purse. "Nothing," she says. "Just a list. In case I forget one of the ingredients."

"Oh. I thought maybe it was a recipe. You know, like the one from class yesterday."

"You think I need a recipe to make *chang shou mian*?" my mother sniffs.

"No," I say. "But Chef Antonio's recipe was really good, don't you think?"

"It wasn't authentic," she says with a shrug. "But it was . . . interesting."

My father actually pokes his head out from behind his newspaper. When it comes to complimenting other people's cooking, "interesting" is about as generous as Mama gets.

My mother leaves for the store, and my father gets up for a fresh cup of coffee. I smile to myself, feeling like I've won some kind of prize. My mother may not be grilling up hamburgers or making macaroni and cheese (yet), but following a recipe that wasn't handed down for fifty generations is a step in the right direction. A baby step, maybe, but definitely a step.

I'm still smiling when I reach for the last *you tiao* and discover that my father has the same idea. We laugh and split it. Baba folds up his newspaper at last and dunks his *yo tiao* in his coffee before taking a bite. I've never seen him do that before, but it looks pretty tasty, so I dunk mine in what's left in Katie's mug. Not bad. I'm really glad that at least my father can see that Chinese and American traditions make a good mix sometimes.

# CHAPTER 25
## *Liza*

You know that old saying "Time flies"? Well, it must be true because this week totally had wings. On Sunday night I called my dad like always and told him about cooking class and how Mom practically scolded Chef Antonio for not including Nana's kugel as one of his examples. I said she actually threatened to make one and bring it to class next week, and Dad said she needs the practice because when he comes for Museum Night at my school, he's going to make

Nana's kugel too, and we'll have a taste-off with me as the judge. I told him that sounded like fun to me, but I didn't say that for Mom . . . not so much.

When my dad comes to visit, he always tries to set up some work meetings, too. If he turns a visit with me and Cole into a business trip, his company pays for it and he can stay at the Marriott in downtown Brooklyn instead of crashing with one of his old friends (which is kind of weird for him, since most of his old friends are friends with Mom). I like when he stays at the Marriott because it has a big pool, but it always feels strange to say good night at the end of the day and go home to our apartment without him. Before we hung up the phone, Dad told me he'd officially booked his room and I should get ready for him to beat me at the backstroke. This is an old joke—my dad can keep himself afloat, but he's never really bothered to learn how to swim—but it's funnier now that he actually lives near the beach.

Back to time flying: Frankie, Lillian, and I worked

on our project three afternoons this week, and we're making a lot of progress. Not enough for Frankie, of course, but she's on some kind of mission to put everyone else's projects to shame and blow Mr. McEnroe away with her creative genius.

I don't know if it's because she's making an effort for me or she's actually starting to like Lillian, but Frankie has been less . . . well . . . Frankie-ish lately when the three of us are together. She and Lillian are far from BFFs, but at least I don't feel like a referee anymore every time we're all in the same room. I'm not sure what will happen when this project is over, but to be honest, it's been nice to hang out with someone other than Frankie sometimes—someone whose personality doesn't "fill the room," as my mom says—and I hope Lillian and I will stay friends, even if it goes against Frankie's grand plan for the universe.

So now it's Saturday, and my mom is checking on Nana's kugel in the oven and getting Cole ready for his "*abuelita* time." That's what Angelica calls the time they spend together at the cooking studio while Mom and I are in class, only Cole can't pronounce *abuelita* so he just squeals, "*Bita* time! *Bita* time!" while my mom attempts to stuff him into his jacket and tie his shoes.

The kitchen smells so good, I could practically take a bite out of the air. This is actually the third time this week that my mom has made a meal from scratch. After we finished off our leftovers from last Saturday's noodle class, Mom got inspired to make her down-home mac 'n' cheese (heaven in a dish) and a lasagna that was almost as good as Frankie's dad's. So what if we've been carbo-loading all week? My mom's getting her cooking groove back, and she's been less moody. I actually heard her singing in the kitchen this morning. It's all good by me.

On the way to class, I carry the kugel while my mom pushes Cole's stroller. She's walking fast, "like a genuine New Yorker," Dad would say, and it's hard to keep up with oven mitts on my hands and carrying a heavy, hot casserole. Mom's never been in this much of a hurry to get to cooking class before, but I'm not complaining—and neither is my brother, who's still babbling about "*bita* time" and bouncing in his seat.

We've never been early to the studio before, but I guess there's a first time for everything. Luckily, Angelica's already here, and Cole practically bursts out of his stroller like the Incredible Hulk when he sees her. Javier's here too, and it looks like he's brought some of his old toy cars for Cole to play with. His usual bored look is replaced by a goofy but sort of sweet smile when he sees how happy his hand-me-downs make my brother. Minus the headphones and attitude, I can see how someone might think Javier was kind of cute. I've caught Lillian staring at him a few times during class, and by the look on her face, I'm pretty sure she has at least a teeny-tiny crush on him. And she *did* get pretty embarrassed when Frankie teased her about him.

"Welcome! *Buenos días!*" Chef Antonio says as the rest of the class arrives. Frankie's mom is chatting with Dr. Wong as they walk in, and while I can't even begin to imagine what they have in common, Lillian's mom actually looks interested in whatever it is they're talking about. Frankie and Lillian walk in behind them looking as surprised as I am that their moms are hitting it off.

Henry and Errol and the Newlyweds come in together too. I guess since the rest of us knew one another already, the four of them just bonded.

"I like to call this class 'Bean Me Up, Scotty,' because today we are exploring the wild and wonderful world of legumes!" Chef announces as we take our seats at the big steel table. "And do you know what else is special about this class? When we are finished, you can say that you've *'Bean there, done that'*!"

We all groan, but Chef Antonio is so nice that we can't help smiling anyway. Well, maybe not

Javier—over in the corner he's just hunching his shoulders and slouching down in his seat and probably wishing he'd put his earphones in before his dad made that awful joke. Even Lillian's mom is grinning a little, though it's possible she didn't appreciate Chef's lame attempt at humor.

"Okay, okay, no more bean jokes—I promise!" Chef Antonio puts his hand over his heart like he's saying the Pledge of Allegiance. "How about a little history of the legume instead? Seeds of the plant family—beans, peas, lentils, soybeans, and peanuts—go a long way back. They were found in the royal tombs of Egypt, mentioned in Homer's *Iliad* and the Old Testament, and grown by the Aztecs, the Incas, the native peoples of North America, and early farmers in Afghanistan and the Himalayan foothills."

*Wow.* And I've always thought of them as a side dish. Chef dips his hand into a bowl of dried beans on the table and lets them sift through his fingers. "Did you know that beans like these are believed to have saved medieval Europe from starvation?"

Chef Antonio makes that last part sound totally serious, and we all lean in a little closer, hoping there's more to the story. Who knew beans could be so interesting?

"Speaking of starvation, *amigos*," Chef says, "let's get cooking!"

Everyone laughs, and my mom, who happens to be sitting right next to Chef Antonio, gives him a playful shove. It reminds me of something she would do with my dad, and Chef is smiling at her just the way Dad would. Is my mom flirting with him?

"Oh, but wait!" Chef says, noticing our foil-covered casserole dish for the first time. "It looks like *nuestra amiga* Jackie has brought something for show-and-tell." He looks at my mom. "What have we here?"

My mom looks slightly embarrassed as she peels off the foil, revealing a perfect noodle kugel. Even

Dad would be impressed. "This is Nana Silver's noodle kugel."

She hands Chef Antonio a fork that we brought from home, and he takes a bite right from the pan. He closes his eyes as he chews, as if he's concentrating hard with his taste buds.

"*Dios mío,*" Chef says, opening his eyes at last. "Nana is a genius. I must have her recipe."

My mother gives him one of her "Don't I know it?" smiles. "I'll have to think about it because, normally, you have to marry into the family to get it," she says. "And only if you promise to include it the next time you teach a noodle class."

Chef Antonio makes an X over his heart with his finger. "Promise."

We make a spicy Indian lentil stew called *daal*, Mexican refried beans (which you don't actually fry twice), and Native American succotash with lima beans, green beans, and corn. They all taste better than they sound, but I'm not very hungry.

Something about the way my mom and Chef Antonio have been looking at each other gives me a funny feeling in my stomach. It's the only time I can remember cooking class—or Chef Antonio—making me lose my appetite.

# CHAPTER 26
*Frankie*

Coming home today, I feel pretty good. Not only did Mr. Mac call on me not once, not twice, but *three* times—*and* tell me that I have an ear for history (or just for him, but if that's what he thinks, excellent!)— but Liza, Lillian, and I are golden for our project.

Since working at our houses has been fairly disastrous, on Monday we asked the nice art teacher, Ms. Lu, if we could stay in at lunch and work in her room. She was totally cool with it, so we've been spending our lunchtime there every day this week. And we rock! We've cranked out a papier-mâché ice-cream cone. (An ancient food, ice cream, brought to this country by lots of different immigrant groups, because I guess everyone likes creamy frozen sweetness! Plus, it's such a melting-pot example, since the ice-cream cone was supposedly invented at the St. Louis World's Fair in 1904. Melting-pot food and history—a perfect combination.) Then we finished our bagel diorama and another one on the hot dog. They are so cute! We're not finished, but we're in great shape.

So I'm walking down my block, definitely singing a happy tune in my head, when I see Dad up ahead of me—by himself with Rocco on a leash. How lucky am I? This week Dad's off on Thursday, making today even better. When I catch up to him, he gives me a one-armed hug.

"Hey, hon! School's out already? Seems so early. Don't they teach you guys anything?" My dad loves to tease, and somehow, he's convinced that if he says something often enough, it will get funnier.

"Ha-ha, Dad. We're there plenty of time, believe me. And, I'll have you know, it was stupendous today—one of my teachers even said so."

He stands up from picking up Rocco's poop with a plastic bag, then tries to ruffle my hair. "Gross, Dad, keep away from me!"

Shaking his head, he starts up our stoop. "Hysterical much, Frankie? My hand was encased in plastic, goofy girl. So I guess you don't want to go get stuff for dinner with me?"

I jump at the chance to go shopping with my dad. It's so fun to watch him make his choices at the butcher shop, inspect the fruit and vegetables at the produce stand, sniff deeply and dramatically in the bakery to make the perfect bread selection, and then, if we still need something else, talk to all the old ladies at the supermarket as we pick up the rest. It's kind of an adventure. And they all worship him. As my dad likes to say, the world loves a fireman.

"Definitely!" I run up behind him. He chuckles and leans inside to deposit Rocco, douse himself with hand sanitizer, and grab some shopping bags from the hooks in the hall. "Let's hit it, Frankie!"

I dump my backpack inside and follow him back out the door.

We make our way down Court and Smith Streets, stopping every few feet to chat or check on one person or another. First it's someone my dad went to high school with, then it's a friend of my grand-mother's. A girl who used to babysit us who's visiting from college, then a guy from my dad's fire company. Every day is old home week when you've lived your whole life in Brooklyn.

At Esposito's, the butcher shop, he's waved to the front of the line—and since it's Dad, nobody seems to mind. He points to some pork chops, which the plump man behind the counter wraps up for him right away, congratulating him on his choice and throwing in an extra one or two—for all those growing boys, he says. Pointing the wax-paper package at me, the butcher booms, "This your girl, Joe? She don't look nothing like you—she's beautiful!"

I blush and shove my hands in my pockets. So embarrassing. But everybody laughs—the guy has said the same thing every time we've come in since I can remember. I used to love it, but now I'm mortified.

"Looks just like her mama, Dom, just like her mama." Dad smiles. He gives them a friendly salute. "Later, fellas."

Now we head to the Korean vegetable stand, where he'll probably get a bunch of bitter greens to cook up with garlic and some little potatoes.

I've been telling him about my day and about the exciting progress we're making with our food project. Watching his confidence with tonight's ingredients reminds me of something.

"Hey, Dad, do you know what you're going to make for the Museum Night potluck? Granny's gnocchi maybe? Or that seven fishes thing?"

Poking the dusty potatoes with one finger and balancing the good ones in his other hand, he doesn't even look up. "Oh right, yeah. I haven't even thought about it, *bella*. When is it again? Week after next?"

"No, Dad! It's Monday. You know that already; I put it on the master calendar."

Turning suddenly, Dad drops all the potatoes he's juggling. "Monday? As in this coming Monday?"

"Um, yeah. Monday. Same date it's been for the last month or so." I crack myself up. Doesn't anyone listen to me? I cannot take my eyes off some purple peppers and think that Chef Antonio would really like to see these.

Despite years of practice, I'm not prepared for what comes next. Dad squints his hazel eyes, like he's in pain.

"Francesca, I am so sorry." Uh-oh. Full name, serious tone, this is not going to end well.

"Uh, what's wrong?" I stall.

"Hon, next week I have that training trip. I told you guys, I'll be gone for a few days. Remember?"

You know that expression about blood running cold, or turning to ice, or whatever it is? That happens to me right now. All the liquid in my body freezes, and I cannot move my limbs. Somehow, I manage to squeak something in spite of my clenched jaw.

"But, *Dad*, you cannot be serious. You promised. I *put it* on the *calendar!*"

"Frankie, I guess I forgot to look at the calendar. I'm so sorry, baby. It only works if we remember to check that thing, and anyway, this is beyond my control. It's required training. We have to stay up-to-date with new technology, you know that. It's my job."

When have I heard that one before? Oh yeah, all my life.

"But the calendar . . . the potluck . . . ," I begin to whine.

"We'll figure out something, Francesca. I

promise. It will be okay. Maybe, thanks to your cooking class, Mom will be able to pull something together!" He grins to himself before picking the potatoes back up and sauntering to nice Mr. Pak, the grocer, to ring him up. I'm still frozen in the aisle, unable to do more than sputter.

My mom? *My* mom will have to make a traditional Italian dish for everyone at school to share? Everyone? At school? To actually eat? If both my grandmothers weren't out of town right now—one in Florida, the other in Italy—I would ask one of them to do it. They had to pick *now* to be away? *My mom* bringing something she made to a school event. This so can*not* be happening.

My good day is now just a memory. My nightmare has begun.

# CHAPTER 27
## *Lillian*

It's hard to believe that today is our last cooking class. It's pathetic, I know, but American Cooking 101 has been the closest thing I've had to a social life since we moved to Brooklyn. What's going to happen next week, after the Immigration Museum project is over? My "Frankie project" has actually started showing signs of success—she hasn't been openly mean to me in a couple of weeks, and lately she's been acting almost friendly. Once our social studies assignment is complete, will she go back to treating me like an annoying nobody? Will Liza still be my friend, or will she decide it's too much trouble trying to stick up for me around Frankie when we don't have to work together anymore?

So many questions are jostling around in my head, but there's no time to think about them too much right now because my mother and I are running late for class. Well, not late, but definitely not as punctual as she likes to be. Today's theme is bread, probably the one food other than cheese that my mother has no interest in or use for. (I, of course, can't get enough of it.) There's plenty of bread in China, but it's usually more like Wonder Bread than the homemade kind you get from bakeries in America and other countries. My mother has definitely never baked bread— or probably even wanted to—so she was in no hurry to leave for the cooking studio today.

When we finally get to class, it looks like Chef Antonio is delaying his introduction to finish some prep work. Normally, this would have frustrated my mother, but today I'm the one who's annoyed. I thought my mother was beginning to appreciate these cooking classes, maybe even enjoy them a little, but the fact that she's literally dragging her feet this afternoon makes me wonder if there was ever any point to this whole experiment.

"Ah, *bueno, bueno!*" bellows Chef Antonio as we grab our aprons and take the two empty seats at the end of the table. "I am just getting everything *perfecto* for our last—and most challenging—class." He stops to wink at my mother. "I know how much our MeiYin enjoys a challenge."

My mother's lips turn up into a half smile, and I can tell that she's embarrassed. She definitely enjoys a challenge when she can be pretty sure she's going to win. Noodles or peppers? No problem. Beans? Bring 'em on. But bread? Bread is uncharted territory, and when it comes to food, my mother is used to knowing her way.

Chef tells us that the history of bread goes back thousands and thousands of years—at least ten thousand. But archaeologists have found evidence of flour dating back thirty thousand years, so people may have baked bread then, too. He says bread of some kind might be the only food that can be found in every single cuisine in the world—yes, even Chinese. One of the earliest types of bread was flat bread, like pita, tortillas, chapatis, and loads of other kinds that are still popular in many cultures. Eventually, people figured out that yeast made dough rise, which meant fluffier bread, and that's when loaf breads started becoming popular.

Baking loaf breads takes time, because you have to let the dough sit for it to rise. Today we're making baguettes, those long French breads that call out to you when you pass by a bakery window. Chef Antonio says baguettes are tricky because you have to let the dough rise in stages, but a fresh baguette is *el mejor*—the very best—and he can never teach a bread class without including them.

The first thing we do is combine water, yeast, and flour, and my mother actually lets me handle the mixing. We have to wait twenty minutes for the flour to soak up the water, so we start on our second recipe: popovers. Chef says popovers are the American version of the British Yorkshire pudding. I've never had either one, so I have no idea how they're supposed to turn out. From the skeptical look on her face, I can tell my mother doesn't know either—it's a look that says, if something is unfamiliar, it must be inferior.

It turns out making popovers is easy—or at least mixing the batter is. All you do is blend butter, flour, salt, eggs, and milk and pour the mixture into an already-hot muffin or popover pan. Then you stick it in the oven for forty minutes. Chef Antonio told us if we've never had popovers, we're going to be surprised—but absolutely no peeking!

While the popovers are baking, we all go back to the baguettes. Just salt the dough a little, and it's time for kneading. When my cousin Chloe and I were little, we were obsessed with Play-Doh. We loved to form it into balls and then roll it out with our little plastic rolling pins. Or we'd twirl it between our palms to make long tubes that we'd stuff into a special Play-Doh press. When you squeezed the handle, your funny-looking tubes would magically be transformed into perfectly even ropes of hearts or stars.

The dough for our baguettes is even more fun to knead than Play-Doh, and it doesn't have that Play-Doh-y smell. I'm really getting into it. My mother, on the other hand, can't quite get the hang of it. There's a rhythm to kneading, and Mama doesn't have that patience. I look around—the class is about even with people who like to knead and people who don't. The Newlyweds are enjoying it, and Henry is too. Errol seems completely perplexed and has moved to a total observer position. Liza and her mom are laughing while kneading their dough, which is definitely taking shape. Chef Antonio has rushed over to Frankie and her mom, which means something has gone terribly wrong.

As for Mama, her dough is lumpy and cracking, and she has a look on her face to match. My mother is zero fun when she's grumpy, so I instinctively put down my own dough and pick up hers. I sprinkle a fresh layer of flour on her board and then begin to knead her dough.

"Like this, Mama," I say, and I show her how I lean into the dough with the heels of my hands.

When the lumps and cracks are gone, I look up at her. My mother is gazing at me in a way I don't recognize. I'm not sure what she's thinking, but I decide not to worry about it. "Now you try."

After a moment of hesitation my mother shrugs and presses her hands into her dough. Not bad. I get back to work on my own, and soon we're kneading in sync, our almost-identical hands making the same movements at exactly the same time. My mother raises her eyebrows and looks me in the eye.

"Interesting" is all she says. I decide to take it as a compliment.

It's time to let our dough rise, but our popovers aren't ready to be taken out of the oven yet. So Chef gets us started on our last recipe: naan, a flat bread that's popular in many Middle Eastern and South Asian countries. He tells us that naan is normally made in the oven, but we're going to make a stove-top version instead that's faster and, he promises, just as tasty.

In a bowl we mix together flour, sugar, and baking soda, then add plain yogurt. I am excited that there's kneading involved in this recipe too, and I notice that my mother watches me get my dough going before starting on her own.

A loud buzzer sounds, and everyone stops what they're doing and looks up at Chef Antonio. "It's time!" he announces, and we all abandon our naan dough to race over and gather around the big oven. Even Javier joins the crowd, peeking over his father's shoulder as Chef carefully slides the five pans onto the cooling rack with his big oven-mitted hands.

Wow. Popovers really do look like they've popped—or they're about to, anyway. They're like golden dough balloons bursting out of little muffin bottoms. Each group of two has a different color popover pan. Ours is red, the Chinese color for good fortune—I bet you can guess who chose it! I'm thrilled, and a little amazed, to discover that the entire red pan of popovers is perfectly glowing and puffy. My mother also looks surprised—and impressed. She takes in the perfection of our popovers, then looks up at me, and there's something in her expression that I've seen before—only it's usually the result of her culinary achievements, not mine. I think it might be pride.

The popovers in the green pan have gone flat. Or maybe they never even popped. It's not hard to guess which pair the green pan belongs to. Frankie and her mom look as deflated as their popovers.

Maybe they'll have better luck with the baguettes.

Our popovers taste as good as they look—maybe even better. The crust around the "balloon" is crisp and light, while the bottom is moist and deliciously buttery. I can see why the British call their version "pudding." We have to eat quickly because it's time to flatten and fold our baguette dough and then put it back in an unheated oven to rise again. Chef Antonio says there won't be enough time to wait for it, so he gives us each an identical mound of dough that has already risen to do the next steps. I look over at Frankie as she happily exchanges her bowl of dough for a new one. If her mom had any trouble following the recipe, Chef's replacement could be their lucky break.

Before we form our baguettes, we have to grill our naan. Each group gets a special frying pan called a *tava*, which we start heating before anything goes in it. Then we divide our dough into balls and roll them out with a rolling pin. Naan doesn't need to be a perfect circle, but I'm excited when mine turns out pretty symmetrical anyway. My mother rolls hers too thin, like a dumpling wrapper. I help her mold it back into a ball and then roll it out again, thicker this time. I'm used to helping Mama with some stuff in the kitchen, but I'm usually the one learning from her. It seems like now our roles are reversed. I wonder if this is as weird for her as it is for me.

We brush our naan with ghee—a special kind of butter—and lay it in the hot pan. As the dough heats up, it starts to bubble. The room is pretty quiet while everyone concentrates on the naan, not wanting to flip it too soon, but also hoping it doesn't burn. I make eye contact with Liza, who's three stoves away, and mouth the words, *This is so cool!*

*Totally!* she mouths back.

I help my mother turn over our naan, and the bubbles sizzle as they hit the pan. When our naan puffs up like a pita, we flip it again, and in less than a minute it's done. I tear off a piece and take a bite.

Mmmm. It's crispy on the outside, chewy on the inside, and just the right amount of salty. Even my mother, the bread-o-phobe, can't stop at just one bite.

Chef Antonio says there's just enough time to turn our dough into baguettes and bake them before class is over. He shows us how to divide our dough into three equal parts and shape each piece into a long rope that will become a baguette. Usually, Chef explains, the dough would need to rise again, but he used a special yeast so we can put them straight into the oven. In the time it takes me to make two ropes, my mother makes one, and I'm pretty sure we both notice that mine are smoother and more even than hers. Before they go in the oven, we use a sharp knife to make diagonal slits along the length of each baguette, and even though she never lets me touch her knives at home, this time Mama lets me do all of the cutting.

While our baguettes are baking, Chef Antonio calls us all back to the table. Normally, we spend the last half hour of class cleaning up, but today he tells us not to bother—he'll do it after we go home. He pulls up an extra stool next to his and calls Javier over to join us.

"*Mis amigos*, sharing my knowledge about the origins of some American food with you has been such a pleasure. I hope you enjoyed our little Saturday cooking club as much as I have and maybe learned a few things about your favorite dishes as well!" He looks from Liza to Frankie to me. "And I want to say a special *gracias* to you three girls, for allowing me to be a part of this very nice mother-daughter activity you planned." Chef puts his arm around Javier's shoulders and tousles his curls until Javier pushes his hand away. "There's nothing more important than time with family, and you girls have shown me that even big kids can survive spending a few hours a week with their parents. *Muchas gracias* for that. You inspired me to find something like this to do with *mi hijo*."

Javier raises his eyebrows, and my stomach does a little flip. "Oh, man," he sighs.

Everyone laughs. The buzzer goes off. Our baguettes look professional—all of them. Chef passes around little dishes of butter, and we all devour our bread until we can't possibly swallow another bite—including Frankie and her mom, whose baguettes look (and sound) more like breadsticks, and my mother, who seems to have decided that she's a bread person, at least for today. I tear off a piece of our last loaf and offer it to Javier, who smiles and holds out his hand. When I give it to him, I'm pretty sure that at least one of my fingers touches one of his.

# CHAPTER 28
## *Liza*

Tanya, our gym teacher, talks about karma. When she's not teaching middle school kids, she's a yoga instructor at one of those yoga studios in Manhattan that you read about celebrities going to. Tanya says she's a student of "Eastern philosophies," and she told us karma is basically the law of cause and effect: If you put positive stuff out into the world, you're going to get positive stuff back. The same goes for the negative stuff. It's probably bad karma to say this, but for the first time, I think I understand why my mom divorced my dad. Or at least I understand one of the reasons. Right now I sort of want to divorce him too.

Yesterday, before we all said good-bye and left cooking class for the last time, Frankie, Lillian, and I told Chef Antonio that we had finally decided what we were going to make for our Immigration Museum exhibit: bagels. We all love them, they're totally New York City and part of the whole melting-pot food tradition, and we have an amazing diorama to go along with them, thanks to Lillian's incredible art skills. We thought Chef would think it was a great idea too, but instead, he shook his head.

"With the right recipe, homemade bagels are delicious, *chicas*, but they're very difficult to make. And they take so long—there are so many steps. Just to start, the dough needs a lot of time to rise, even more than was needed for our baguettes. When did you say this school event is happening?"

"Monday night," all three of us said at once. We've been working toward it for so long, we could probably all recite the date in our sleep.

Chef shook his head some more. Not a good sign. "*Ay*, no, no, no. Bagel dough needs to rise in the refrigerator overnight. You'd have to start right now. Then tomorrow you'd still need to let the dough sit at room temperature for an hour, shape the bagels, boil them, and *then* bake them. But then they would be stale, day-old bagels for your big party, and that won't be very tasty. I'm sorry, *hijas*, but I think it's time to come up with a Plan B, as Javi likes to say."

Plan B? It took a month for us to agree on our Plan A! Frankie, Lillian, and I must have looked as depressed as I felt, because Chef Antonio suddenly went into crisis intervention mode.

"Chins up, *chicas*!" he practically commanded. "Bagels are bread, right? And we just had our bread class! You're all experts at the baguette now, why don't you make a few of those for your presentation?"

Everyone in the class nodded their heads and said things like, "Great idea!" and "Problem solved!" Everyone except the three of us, that is.

"It has to be something that people think of as an 'American' food," Frankie said in a really flat voice. "Everybody knows baguettes are from France."

Chef shrugged, ignoring her tone. "Okay, so no baguettes. But don't worry, I'm full of ideas. Isn't that right, Javier?"

Javier rolled his eyes.

Chef Antonio ignored him. "Let's see. . . . Naan is too Indian, ciabatta's too Italian. . . . Scones?"

Frankie shook her head. "Too English."

"*Es verdad,*" Chef said. "This is true. Well, then, how about rolls? You could do pumpernickel rolls, hamburger rolls, sourdough rolls—"

Lillian's head snapped up. She didn't look depressed anymore. "I love sourdough rolls!" she squealed in a very un-Lillian-like way. "But sour-dough is from San Francisco, right? Like me."

Chef smiled and winked at Lillian. "Ah, well, this is the interesting thing about the history of a country of immigrants, right, *niña*? It's true that sourdough—like you—arrived in New York and the rest of America from San Francisco. But your family came to California from China, right?"

Lillian nodded.

"Well, sourdough wasn't born in this country either. It was brought to northern California by bak-ers from France. But the French did not invent sour-dough any more than the San Franciscans did. People across Europe had been using a sourdough starter to make bread for many centuries. And—how do you like this, *amiga*?—even the Egyptians were making sourdough way back in 1500 B.C.!"

"Wow," Lillian said. "You really know a lot about food." Even Dr. Wong looked impressed.

"That's because I always did my homework,"

Chef Antonio said, giving Javier's shoulder a squeeze. "If you do your homework, you'll know a lot about all sorts of things."

Javier cupped his hands around his mouth. "Wikipedia," he whispered, looking at us. We all laughed—except for Chef, who just looked confused.

"Anyway," he said, "if you girls would like to make sourdough rolls, you have to use a special sourdough starter that takes about three days to mature."

Lillian frowned. "There goes that idea."

"And I just happen to have a jar of it in the refrigerator!"

"Really?" Lillian clapped her hands and practically jumped up and down. "Let's do it!" she squealed, and then looked at Frankie and me. "I mean, what do you guys think?"

"I think it's a great idea," I said, looking at Frankie. "I'd rather do bagels, but it sounds like we really don't have time. And we want to have enough time to do a great job. Okay with you, Franks?" I gave her my best puppy-dog eyes.

Frankie looked from me to Lillian and back again. "Fine," she said, shrugging. "Whatever."

Lillian started in on the clapping again. I've definitely never seen her so excited. Who knew sourdough rolls could make someone so happy? She must really be homesick.

"*Perfecto!*" Chef exclaimed. "And since the starter is already in the refrigerator, why don't you make the rolls right here in the studio tomorrow? I come here many Sundays anyway to do some prep work for my show, so it's no *problema.*"

And so that's where we're heading now, as soon as Frankie gets here to pick me up. Lillian's mom offered to give us both a ride, but Frankie made up some excuse about errands she had to do on the way and how she needed me to help her. After six weeks of working on the project together, I really don't know what she has against Lillian, but apparently, she still can't get over it. She's in a better mood about one thing: Her dad stayed up all night before he left to make some amazing Italian food. So she knows she's bringing something impressive—and edible!—to the potluck.

This morning started out great. I was looking forward to making the very last (and most fun) part of our project and getting to spend even more time with Chef Antonio, who seems more like a really cool . . . I don't know . . . uncle to me now than a cute celebrity on TV. My mom seemed happy too—she was making poached eggs and asparagus for breakfast, to go with what was left of our baguettes—and even Cole was acting about as adorable as a two-year-old can with yogurt in his hair and banana all over his face.

And then my dad called.

He was supposed to be getting on a plane this morning and landing in New York before dark. Mom even invited him to have dinner with all of us at the apartment, instead of Dad taking Cole and me out somewhere. She even went grocery shopping on the way home from class yesterday. (I think she wants to show him that in spite of everything, she's back to her old self in the kitchen again—at least when she has time to go to the store.) But my dad wasn't calling from the plane. He wasn't even at the airport.

"I'm really sorry, pumpkin," he told me. "I had to cancel my trip. A big meeting was just scheduled out here for tomorrow, and it's just too important for me to miss."

More important than my big social studies project, apparently. And more important than me.

"You understand, don't you, Lize?"

"Sure," I told him. And like I said, for the first time since he moved away, I guess I do.

"I'll make it up to you, I promise. When you come out here, you can make some of your new recipes for me. That'll be fun, right?"

"Uh-huh," I said. Loads.

# CHAPTER 29
## *Frankie*

It's almost time for the Immigration Museum—finally. I'm so nervous about tonight, I can hardly focus. Mr. Mac gave us one last period to work on our projects, but Liza, Lillian, and I are already finished, so we offered to help other groups. Or Liza and Lillian did—I'm not that generous, except when Mr. Mac asked me to move chairs and supplies around. That I did happily.

The final bell just rang, and all of the seventh

graders are setting up in the social studies corridor, with several rooms devoted to all our projects and the hallway between them taken over for the potluck. Liza, Lillian, and I already dragged a table to the prime corner spot we'd staked out in one of the rooms, so we've done all we can do for now. All of our work is ready to go at my house, just a few blocks from school. No way we're leaving it here, unattended, before the event starts. Who knows what damage could be done?

Liza, Lillian, and I walk out together. There's time to go home, change if we want (I thought we should wear costumes from the immigrant groups whose foods we're highlighting, but Liza and Lillian voted me down), pick up our parents, and meet back here at six thirty.

Then we're going to rock the house.

Liza blows those little hairs out of her eyes and reviews the plan again. "Okay. If all goes well, my mom should already be home whipping up her pecan pie. She promised to leave early to make it fresh. Lillian, all you have to do is get here, and I'm sure your mom has made some kind of amazing Chinese feast, right? And, Franks, you're going to bring the dioramas *and* the sourdough rolls—you sure you can handle all that by yourself?"

I nod. I like a girl who wants to synchronize watches and confirm battle plans.

"Yep," I assure her. "All the pieces are just where we left them yesterday. Boxed up under the stairs. And I put that giant bakery box full of our rolls in a place where no one's going to bother them and Rocco can't reach them, even if he tries: the oven. Perfect, right? My dad's away, so no one's going to use it, and they won't get smashed or eaten, either. I made a huge, impossible-to-miss sign and taped it to the oven door: 'Keep Out on Pain of Death.' Even The Goons won't miss that. All I have to do is defrost the homemade gnocchi that Dad made before he left, pack up the granny cart with the stuff, and wheel it all over here."

We've come to the block where Liza goes one way to get the bus, Lillian goes another way to hop on the train, and I walk one last block home. If it were just Liza and me, we would do this goofy fist-bump-handshake routine that we made up in third grade. It ends with a musical *"holla,"* and we always do it for luck. But there's no way we're teaching it to Lillian, so we just sort of stand around awkwardly for a minute and then wave good-bye.

"See you back at school!" I shout. And they both give me a thumbs-up as they walk away—almost in unison, so I decide their double thumbs-up means good luck.

I'm contemplating what to wear tonight as I push open the front door. We have gazillions of Italia T-shirts around the house in every color and size. I could wear one of those with my denim skirt, tights, and boots. Or would Liza and Lillian say that was violating the no-costumes rule?

As soon as I walk in, I stop caring about my

wardrobe. Something is wrong—terribly wrong. The house is foggy, and a horrible scorched smell assaults me as I run toward the kitchen. Dad's off on his fire training trip, so did the The Goons decide to burn the house down?

I plow through the kitchen door. It's worse than I thought. Much worse. The kitchen reeks of smoke and the oven door is wide open. Our rolls. Our precious rolls that we lovingly mixed and kneaded and baked all day yesterday. The rolls that were supposed to blow Mr. McEnroe—and, you know, everyone else—away. The rolls that Liza and Lillian entrusted to me. The rolls that were the key to my "awesomeness" are buried in an avalanche of foam, presumably from the mini fire extinguisher currently in my brother Leo's hands. Of course we have one conveniently located in the kitchen—my dad is a firefighter, after all.

For possibly the first time ever, I'm speechless. I am choking on words and screams and sobs that are duking it out in my throat to see what comes out first. If I weren't leaning on the doorframe, I think I might collapse.

I realize that Mom, Leo, and Nicky are all looking at me. My mom, who must see the homicidal glint in my eyes as I glare at Goon Number One, rushes toward me.

"Francesca, sweetheart, it was me. It was all *my* fault. I am so, so sorry, honey. I am so sorry."

She leads me to a chair, and I am trying to process her words. Of course it's all her fault. There's an oven involved. Why wouldn't it be?

She strokes my hair back from my face while my brothers just stare at me. I must look really scary, because neither of them is saying anything—at all. Highly unusual.

Mom kneels down next to me. "I was trying to be helpful. When Nicky and I got home, I took Dad's gnocchi out of the freezer and put the oven on. I was opening the peanut butter jar for Nicky at the same time, so I just shoved the gnocchi on the top rack without really looking and went downstairs to do some laundry. While I was down there, I smelled the smoke and heard Nicky scream. When I got back to the kitchen, Leo had saved the day with the fire extinguisher. But, um, unfortunately, your rolls got ruined in the process."

She looks nervously at my brother, who seems reluctant to attract my attention by moving, speaking, or even blinking.

"It was a little overkill, I know. I mean, we probably could have salvaged the rolls from the box and definitely the gnocchi. But it was quick thinking on his part, Frankie—he was doing what he thought Dad would have done. And neither of us meant to hurt anything. Or anyone."

When I've finally cleared my throat of all the competing emotions, my voice is actually pretty much under control, given how I feel.

"And what about the ginormous sign that said

'Keep Out'? How did you not see it? The one that said 'On Pain of Death,' because of its precious contents? Did you think for a minute after reading it that maybe turning on the oven or blasting it with toxic foam might *not* be the thing to do?"

Nicky holds up a paper airplane. "This sign, Frankie?" he asks in a voice so small and scared that I actually almost feel bad for him. "I wanted to try the new airplane my friend Julian taught me before I forgot how to make it. So I just grabbed the first piece of paper I saw. I didn't look at what it said." He sort of gulps. "Is this your sign?"

Of course it is. And of course he didn't read it. It wasn't covered with pictures of Greek gods or vehicles or superheroes.

Mom looks miserable. Some other time I might feel sorry for her, but this is not that time. "I should have noticed the bakery box, *bella*, but you know I'm always doing three things at once and forgetting to look both ways. And Leo was just trying to save the day." She smoothes my hair again. "Nobody meant to ruin your snack."

Nicky chimes in. "Or Pop's gnocchi."

*My snack?* That did it. "Snack? Snack? Those rolls were not just a snack, they were an important part of a *group* project for *tonight*! A part of the project we worked really hard on. All day yesterday, remember? There's no way we can make more sourdough in time! You have to have a starter, and . . ." I have to stop. This must be what they call a "panic attack"—I'm having trouble catching my breath and "using my words," as Mom likes to say to Nicky. I just want to scream and punch something—or someone.

It occurs to me that I have to tell Liza and Lillian what happened. They're probably getting dressed right now, thinking that everything is fine, when, in fact, everything is SO. NOT. FINE. And how much will they hate me when they hear about this latest Caputo catastrophe?

I storm out to get my phone. Mom and the boys

are trying to clean up and talking to one another in hushed tones. I'm not sure I can trust my voice, so I decide to text Liza instead. All I can think of to say is one word:

*DISASTER.*

Then, just so she doesn't think I'm in the hospital—although that sounds like an excellent place to be right now—I send another:

*ROLLS DESTROYED.*

Then I send the same message to Lillian.

Liza must not have her phone nearby, but Lillian writes back immediately.

*What happened?*

How can I describe it in a text? I try:

*Fire . . . foam . . . all gone.*

My message has barely gone when she replies:

*We can fix it. Can I come over?*

Fix it? How? Even if I thought it were possible, it would be Liza's help I wanted, not Lillian's. But if Liza's not around, what choice do I have?

*Yes,* I text back.

Then I try calling Liza. She always knows what to do in a crisis. And I need her. On what feels like the hundredth ring, she picks up her phone, all out of breath. I tell her what happened.

First she just says, "Oh my God, oh my God, oh my God."

But then she calms down, and although she doesn't seem mad, exactly, she sounds a little, well, annoyed. She says she wasn't sure the oven was the safest place to store the roles in the first place. This is not what I need to hear right now. *Thanks, Lize. Thanks a lot.*

Also, there's no way she can come over to help me and Lillian, because she's watching Cole while her mom finishes baking. She offers to call us if she comes up with any brilliant ideas, but I tell her we'll just figure something out.

When I hang up, I realize that I appreciate the fact that Lillian was instantly willing to spring into action.

At least she's on her way over, which is more than I can say for Liza.

I take a deep breath and go back into the kitchen. All three of my brothers are here now, cleaning the oven and helping Mom open all the sticky windows. We have less than two hours before we're supposed to be at school, and we have to start from scratch.

The boys take one look at me and leave the room. I guess I have that "storm cloud" look my dad sometimes talks about. My mom looks up from scooping more foam.

"Hey, *bella*. I know you're upset, but let's try to come up with a solution, okay? We can run to Mazzola's and pick up—"

"No," I interrupt her. "We have to make something, that's the whole point. That's why we took the class and everything." My fists are clenched; I'm still having a hard time with "using my words."

"Frankie," Mom says, "whether you make something from scratch or not, the class was worth it. For lots of reasons." She comes over and kisses the top of my head and then looks me right in the eyes. "I may not be a chef yet, but I loved hanging out with my big, brilliant girl for a few hours every week. And we made some new friends."

That's all great, but I cannot think about mother-daughter bonding right now. And you know how when someone's trying to be nice to you while you're upset, it actually makes it harder not to cry? That is totally happening.

"Thanks," I mumble, ducking away from my mom. "But now what do we do?"

The doorbell rings. Lillian must have flown here. I run to the front door, and she's standing there, out of breath, holding her bike. I guess she *did* pretty much fly here. I have to admit I'm happy to see her.

Back in the kitchen Mom gives Lillian a hug. I guess she's happy to see her too.

I tell Lillian exactly what happened and how everything got so messed up. She takes a long look around the room and then turns to me with that calm, kittenlike expression of hers.

"You're right, Frankie, your text did not lie. This is a *disaster.*" On another day that might have made me mad, but somehow, right now, it was the perfect thing to say. We both laugh harder than we should, but it makes total sense.

Mom looks confused, but she's not about to question any improvement in my mood. She claps her hands like the second-grade teacher that she is and says, "Ladies, what can we do to make this right? Is there anything else from your project we can make, anything that might be easy?"

Lillian scrunches up her forehead like she's thinking hard, but I've got nothing. And I'm more than a little worried about my mom using the word "we." I watch her shovel more foam into a garbage bag, which probably also contains the remnants of our rolls and Dad's gnocchi. To stop myself from obsessing over damage that can't be undone, I run to get our carefully packed-up dioramas. Maybe if we look at what we've made, something will strike us. Another big idea would come in handy right about now.

The table is relatively clutter-free, so I spread out all our stuff: the dioramas, the papier-mâché food, the reports and illustrations mounted on poster boards. My mom stops trying to come up with a solution to the disaster (that she was partially responsible for) and takes a good look at our project. "You girls did all that? It's amazing!"

I catch Lillian's eye and we smile. Then Mom asks, "I hate to be dense, but what's the pink thing with the waffle-y base?"

I sigh, not really in the mood to explain. "That's our ice-cream cone, can't you tell? Ice cream was brought to America by a bunch of different immigrant groups—"

Lillian stops my mini-lecture and grabs the papier-mâché cone and practically dances around the room. "That's it! That's what we can do!"

"Huh?" Mom and I both say together.

Lillian is so excited, she squeaks. "We can make the ice-cream cone! I mean, we can buy ice cream and take it in a cooler full of ice—do you guys have a cooler? And who doesn't love waffle cones, right? They may not be exactly like the ones you get at an ice-cream parlor, but we can run out and buy a bunch of boxes of frozen waffles, defrost them, try to flatten them out a bit somehow with a rolling pin or something, maybe fold them into a cone shape to hold a scoop of ice cream?"

That's brilliant. *Totally* brilliant. I can tell my mom thinks so too. "Actually, Lillian, we don't have to buy the waffles," she says. "I'm married to a master waffle maker and we have a waffle iron right here."

Uh-oh, just when I was finally seeing some light at the end of this disastrous tunnel . . . "Um, Mom? Dad is the master waffle maker. *Dad.* And he's not here, remember?"

She puts her hand on my shoulder and leans in

to my scowling face. "Have a little faith, Francesca. I'm going to make the waffles. How about you believe in me, just like I believe in you? Besides"—she winks—"I have a secret weapon this time: you two!"

I look at her for a minute. She raises her eyebrows as if to say, *Well?* Finally, I shrug and throw up my hands. What else can I do? It's a plan. The only plan we have.

She and Lillian start bustling around the kitchen, cracking eggs, sifting flour, plugging in the waffle iron. They seem to really want me to go out and get tons of ice cream, so Mom yells for one of The Goons to help me and the other to come finish cleaning the kitchen. And the amazing thing is that they do. No complaining, no wisecracks, they just do it.

Joey, Nicky, and I take Mom's wallet and run to the grocery store, picking out a bunch of different ice creams and loads of ice. We decide to get flavors like French vanilla and dulce de leche that were invented in other countries—or at least sound like they were. By the time we get home, the kitchen is a waffle factory. Leo has basically removed all evidence of the Catastrophe, and my mom and Lillian are churning out doughy, golden waffles in perfect harmony. While they're still warm from the iron, Lillian artfully folds the waffles and ties them with string in a perfect little bow. Good thing Nicky keeps a giant ball of string around!

Leo found a bunch of large sneaker boxes somewhere that he's lined with wax paper to hold the waffle cones (hopefully, the only sneakers in these boxes were brand new!). My mom, who is covered in flour and still has a little foam in her hair, is more pleased with herself than I've ever seen her look in a kitchen. Only a few of the waffles burned around the edges, and Lillian and I just scrape those bites off. Nobody will ever know.

As for the traditional Italian dish that we're supposed to bring to the potluck, Mom and Lillian are all over that, too. There's always a ton of pasta in our pantry, and Mom has assigned Joey the job of boiling the noodles, which reduces the possibility of injuries. Who knew my brothers were actually this capable? Even Nicky is helping. He found some jars of my dad's famous marinara sauce in the cabinet, so we'll just dump that on the pasta and top it with some fresh basil leaves from the plant Dad always has growing on the windowsill. As Chef Antonio would say, *bueno, bueno.*

Watching Lillian quietly skipping around our kitchen, making little jokes with my brothers, having fun cooking with my mother, and maintaining her cool when I absolutely lost mine, I realize something about her that I probably should have known a long time ago: She's a true friend. She came to my rescue when I was never that nice to her, when I never even wanted her around. But here she is. And, if I haven't completely scared her away, I hope she'll stick around.

# CHAPTER 30
## *Lillian*

My mother parks outside of Frankie's house so we can all walk together to school. When the Caputos (all of them) and I go out to meet her, Frankie's mom wraps her arms around Mama in a big hug. My mother is not a hugger, but not to accept one would be disrespectful, so she hugs back. I have to force myself not to laugh as I watch her smile politely and awkwardly pat Mrs. Caputo—er, Theresa, as she just told me to call her—on the back.

The big bowl my mother is carrying makes the hug even more awkward. It's covered in aluminum foil, and I realize that in my frenzy to get over to Frankie's to help fix the disaster, I didn't even bother to ask what she was making. And now she refuses to tell me what's in the bowl. I could probably figure it out just from the "aroma"—one of Chef Antonio's favorite words—but I think my nostrils might be permanently seared with the smells of smoke and whatever those chemicals are in fire extinguishers.

When we reach Clinton Middle School's big red doors, there's a crowd of seventh graders and their families already filing in, but Liza's nowhere to be seen. I look at Frankie, wondering if we're thinking the same thing: Is Liza going to be late because Cole's babysitter bailed again at the last minute? Is her mom even going to make it? Frankie bites her lip, and I can tell she's worried too. We enter the building with all of the other kids and parents, and we're carried along by the current of bodies like a school of fish, up the flight of stairs and out into the sea of the social studies corridor.

Frankie and I lead our mothers to the potluck area first and settle them in next to each other at one of the tables. Still no sign of Liza and her mom. Mr. McEnroe's here, though, and Frankie immediately turns to him and flashes one of her movie-star smiles. "Good evening, Francesca!" I hear him say in his super-enthusiastic way. "And this must be your mother! I hear the two of you are becoming professional chefs. Can't wait to taste whatever you've got there." Frankie and her mom exchange a look and then burst out laughing. Mr. Mac looks totally confused, but he chuckles with them anyway, just to be polite.

As Frankie's brothers scatter off somewhere, we leave our mothers to chat with the other parents and head to our table to set up our display. As soon as we get there, we both sigh with relief. Liza is waiting for us, along with her mom, who's already poking around another group's exhibit. I don't see Cole anywhere, so it looks like their sitter came through. Frankie and Liza look at each other for a long time. I'm not sure what's been going on between them, but I suspect Frankie was annoyed that Liza wasn't there to help come up with our Plan C this afternoon. For once, I don't feel like the odd one out.

Whatever was up, it looks like they're over it now. First they practically fall into each other's arms in a massive hug, and then they start dancing around and doing that crazy handshake thing. They twist up their arms, snap in sync, high-five, fist-bump, sing *"holla"* . . . and then they do something new. Something totally unexpected. They each reach out one arm and pull me over into a huddle—a big, three-girl hug. "When Museum Night is over, we'll have to teach you the handshake too," Frankie says. Liza squeezes my hand. I picture Sierra and my cousin Chloe; I still miss them like crazy, but right now all I can think about is how much I can't wait to tell them about my new friends.

Liza and Frankie arrange the papier-mâché food, prop up our mounted reports, and set up an iPad running our edited demonstration clips from the cooking class videos while I get the dioramas all ready. My tiny food really did come out well, and I had so much fun making it. Maybe I'll be a sculptor someday instead of an illustrator or graphic designer. Or, who knows? Maybe I'll be a baker. I was pretty proud of those sourdough rolls, and Frankie's right—these miniature bagels with their almost-microscopic poppy and sesame seeds do look almost real.

Liza is blown away by the waffle cones—especially when she finds out that Frankie's mom was in charge of the waffle iron. She gives us both another hug and apologizes for not being there to make them with us, even though it's not her fault she has to help out with her brother so much. I tell her that at least she made it here, along with her mom, which is really all that matters.

Speaking of mothers, once we're all set up and Frankie and Liza have started scooping ice cream, I go out to the hallway to check on mine. My nostrils must be healing, because it smells incredible out here, and seeing all of this food in one place makes my stomach growl. I realize that it's dinnertime, and with everything that happened today, I haven't eaten anything since lunch, which is at 11:35 for seventh graders. That was a long time ago.

I navigate through the crowd to the table where we left my mother and Theresa. Along the way I notice some of the dishes: Stella Tanaka's dad is there with homemade sushi rolls; a woman who must be Gabriella Perez's grandmother brought tamales that look as good as the ones at the Mexican food truck Sierra and I used to stop at after school; and Alex Vilenchitz's mother made something that looks like pierogi, even though Chef Antonio told us those are from Poland and Alex is Russian.

I find my mother perched over her bowl with

a large spoon in one hand and a chopstick in the other. Now that the bowl is free of its foil, I can see that what she's shoveling out is some kind of noodle dish. The fact that each bite requires lots of slurping tells me she's made longevity noodles—only there's something a bit different about them than usual.

When the crowd around the table finally thins out, I grab a plate and hold it out to my mother. "*Chang shou mian?*" I ask.

She nods.

"It looks funny."

Mama scoops up some noodles and plops them onto my plate, using the chopstick to prevent them from sliding back into the bowl. "Yes, but how does it taste?"

I unwrap a fresh pair of chopsticks from a box on the table and take a bite. It's definitely not my mother's go-to *chang shou mian*, but the flavor is familiar. I take another bite, and suddenly it comes to me where I've tasted this before.

"This is Chef Antonio's recipe!"

My mother smiles slyly, then puts her finger to her lips. "Shhh."

"But you said his recipe wasn't 'authentic.'"

"It isn't," she says. "The spices are different—mostly Chinese, but also a little bit American." She leans in closer. "Just like *you*."

I smile—not a dutiful-daughter smile, but a smile full of genuine warmth and gratitude.

My mother shrugs. "And Chef Antonio's *chang shou mian* tastes good, don't you think?"

I nod. *"Hěn hǎo."* Very good.

I'm about to head back to our exhibit when I feel my mother's hand on my arm.

"I almost forgot," she says, taking three fist-size balls of aluminum foil out of a Ziploc bag and placing them on the table next to the bowl of noodles. "I brought these, too." She unwraps the foil and arranges the three surviving sourdough rolls in a perfect triangle. Yesterday, after we finished baking them,

Liza and Frankie let me take a few home since they reminded me so much of, well, home.

"The Wong family came from China like *chang shou mian*," Mama says, pointing to the pile of noodles on my plate. "But *our* family is from San Francisco, too." My mother tears a piece off one of the rolls, dips it into the sauce on my plate, and takes a bite. She passes the roll to me, and I do the same. It's a strange combination of flavors that you'd never expect to go together, but somehow, it works. Just like us.

# CHAPTER 31
## *Liza*

It's kind of incredible, isn't it—how you can feel like the whole world is against you one minute, and then that you are exactly where you're meant to be the next? Even before the Sourdough Incident, I was seriously dreading the whole Immigration Museum thing. Between six weeks of trying to convince Frankie to play nice with Lillian and my dad canceling his trip at the last minute, I was totally over our project. We'd worked really hard, so I pretended to be excited for the sake of our "team," but when Frankie told me about her mom and brothers totaling our rolls, I pretty much gave up.

Before tonight, the only good things about the last thirty-six hours were baking at the studio with Frankie, Lillian, and Chef Antonio and watching my mom make her pecan pie for the first time since Dad moved away. Even though some of the thickest branches on the family tree hanging over her desk are crocheted with the names of ancestors back in Africa, according to Mom, everything they brought with them was lost when they stepped off the slave ships. She says that her "roots" are in Georgia, where she grew up, and that pecan pie is a traditional food in her family, no matter who invented it.

My mom claims the secret to her recipe is that she buys the pecans raw and toasts them herself. In my mind I can play back memories of her in the kitchen like an episode of a cooking show made just for me: watching her slide a sheet of freshly toasted pecans out of the oven, chop them once they've cooled with her favorite knife, and add them to the gooey mixture of Karo syrup, sugar, butter, and eggs—with a splash of Grandad's favorite bourbon. Seeing my mom take the dusty old Reynolds family cookbook off the shelf for the first time in ages and burst open a bag of fresh pecans was like discovering a DVD you didn't even realize you were missing and pressing the play button. And the way Cole looked at Mom as she moved around the kitchen—singing to herself the way she always used to—like she was an exotic animal at the Prospect Park Zoo, made me want to share my special show with him too.

When I told my mom about our ruined rolls, she said I should go straight over to the Caputos and not to worry about watching Cole. She could keep an eye on him while she baked, and if he got to be a handful, well, showing up to the potluck with a store-bought pie wouldn't be the end of the world. Not the end of hers, maybe, but right at that moment, not having my mom's homemade pecan pie felt pretty close to the End Times. Frankie was on her own for this one. So I lied to my best friend for the first time ever, scooped up my brother, and pulled two stools up to the breakfast bar so that together we could watch Mom work her magic on piecrust and pecans.

By the time the pie was ready, our apartment smelled like Christmas and my mom had changed into a black wraparound dress. She even took the time to touch up her makeup. When Cammy showed up to watch Cole five minutes early, I was actually starting to get excited about the social studies museum. I still hadn't forgiven my dad for choosing a meeting over me, but I was beginning to realize that even without him, I'll always be part of a family. The three of us—Mom, Cole, and me—might not be perfect, but most of the time we're good enough.

It turns out being a group of three is good enough for Frankie too. When she and Lillian walked into the exhibit room, dragging all of our stuff, you would have thought they were BFFs. One of them would start telling a story about Nicky and his paper airplane or describing the taste of fire extinguisher foam, and the other would finish the sentence. If I didn't know them, I'd think they've been friends for two years, instead of two hours. Part of me wishes I'd gone over to help this afternoon after all, so I would know what actually happened that finally brought Frankie and Lillian together. So far all they do when I ask for more details is look at each other and crack up. I guess you had to be there.

Whatever went down at Casa Caputo, Lillian and Frankie—along with Theresa, Nicky, and The Goons—totally killed it with the waffle cones and endless supply of ice cream. Everyone seems impressed with the other parts of our project, too—especially all of the historic details Frankie made sure we included in the dioramas and Lillian's miniature food—but I'm pretty sure our exhibit is so popular because we're the only ones giving out sweets. Mr. McEnroe has been back to "assess" our project three times already, but I've noticed he's less interested in reading the long historical essays on our posters than sampling the different flavors of ice cream.

After the ice cream runs out, the three of us realize that we're starving. We've been so busy scooping and showing off our displays that we haven't even checked out the potluck (except for Lillian, who got around to tasting only what her own mother brought). Out in the hallway we discover that pretty much everything has already been eaten, except for a couple of slices of pizza that Carla DiRosa's parents brought from their restaurant. We're about to divide the two slices up three ways—despite the fact that they're ice cold and the cheese is getting hard—when somebody near the end of the hallway screams. Everyone goes silent, except for the screamer, who, it turns out, is excited rather than in danger.

It's been a day full of surprises, but when Frankie,

Lillian, and I turn around, we find ourselves face-to-face with the biggest surprise of all. Chef Antonio—decked out in his kitchen whites with the ANTONIO'S KITCHEN logo on the side—is walking toward us with a huge grin on his face and a casserole dish in his hands. And he's not alone. Henry, Errol, the Newlyweds, Javier, and even Angelica all make their way over to the table where our mothers are packing up their serving dishes. Ms. Johnson, the security guard, is leading the way, looking totally starstruck. She must be a fan, which explains how they all got in.

"*Buenos noches!* Did we miss the party?" Chef Antonio asks the entire crowd. The kids and parents who watch his show laugh and clap excitedly while everyone else just looks confused. Chef puts his casserole dish down on a table. "I guess nobody's hungry anymore, eh?"

"I am!" Lillian, Frankie, and I blurt out together.

Javier leans, in a somehow cool way, around his dad. "Jinx!"

We all laugh, and I think Lillian might even be blushing.

"I have something here for you, *chicas*," Chef says. "But I'd like this young lady to taste it first." He pulls a fork out of his jacket pocket and hands it to my mom. She looks as stunned as I feel.

Chef Antonio gestures to the casserole dish, and my mom starts peeling away the foil. As soon as she's unwrapped enough to see what's inside, she steps back from the table and pretty much howls. Big, happy laughs like I have not heard from her in forever. Frankie, Lillian, and I look at one another, wondering what Chef could possibly have made that's so funny. Finally, my mom pulls herself together enough to peel away the rest of the foil. It's Nana's noodle kugel. I should have guessed.

Mom wipes the tears out of her eyes and scoops up a forkful of kugel. Chef Antonio watches expectantly as she chews.

"So?" he asks after she swallows.

My mom drags out the moment, slowly licking her lips. "Not bad," she finally says. "Not bad. I think Nana Silver would approve."

Everyone laughs. At least Frankie, Lillian, and I do, along with our moms and everyone from our Saturday cooking club. I look around at all of the now-familiar faces and realize that that's exactly what we are: a big, colorful, mismatched, messy family. And right now that's just what I need.

"*Bueno!*" Chef says, taking a little bow. "*Muy bueno.*"

I have to agree.

# ACKNOWLEDGMENTS

Thanks from both of us to our editor, Fiona, for bringing our tale of three girls, three moms, lots of brothers, several dads, and a couple of grandmothers into the light of day. . . . And to Peter, our tireless agent, for persevering to publication with patience and wisdom.—DAL and JER

My deepest gratitude goes to my coauthor, friend, and neighbor, JillEllyn Riley, for inviting me to join her in dreaming up the adventures of Liza, Frankie, and Lillian at her dining room table, and for never failing to offer me a cup of tea and a plate of cookies. Someday, we will have that cocktail. Much love and thanks to my husband, Ian, for his patience, support, and willingness to take on the role of kid chauffeur while I wrote, and to Lili and Julian for (most of the time) putting up with "Don't go in there, Mommy's working," even on the weekends. Thanks are also due to my own Brooklyn BFFs, for their confidence, counsel, and enthusiasm for early-morning coffee dates.—DAL

Thank you to my coconspirator, Deb Levine, for weathering all manner of crises and craziness—including an earthquake—to keep the cooking club going with grace and a keen sense of humor. To the gifted, creative cooks who contributed delectable ideas for our fictional chef—he is very grateful. To my own dashing fellas, all three—Eóin, Cullen, and Alan—big heart, big love. And as always, to Miles.—JER